Marx Machiavelli Chesterton Emerson Joyce
Abbott Hardy Montaigne Cooper Austen
Defoe Melville Haggard Hugo
Eliot Grimm
Stoker Carroll Christie Molière
Wilde Maupassant Byron
Schiller
Garnett Einstein Fitzgerald Engels Smith
Goethe Hawthorne Kafka
Cotton Dostoyevsky Hall
Baum Kipling Doyle Willis
Leslie Dumas Henry Nietzsche
Flaubert Turgenev Balzac
Stockton Vatsyayana Crane
Burroughs Whitman Verne
Curtis Tocqueville Gogol Vinci
Homer Widger Tolstoy Busch
Darwin Thoreau
Potter Freud Zola Twain Plato Scott
Lawrence
Kant Jowett Stevenson Dickens
Andersen Cervantes Burton Hesse Harte
London Descartes
Poe Aristotle Wells Voltaire
Hale James Hastings Cooke
Bunner Shakespeare
Richter Chambers Irving
Doré Swift Dante Chekhov da Shaw Wodehouse Benedict Alcott
Pushkin
Newton

tredition®

tredition was established in 2006 by Sandra Latusseck and Soenke Schulz. Based in Hamburg, Germany, tredition offers publishing solutions to authors and publishing houses, combined with worldwide distribution of printed and digital book content. tredition is uniquely positioned to enable authors and publishing houses to create books on their own terms and without conventional manufacturing risks.

For more information please visit: www.tredition.com

TREDITION CLASSICS

This book is part of the TREDITION CLASSICS series. The creators of this series are united by passion for literature and driven by the intention of making all public domain books available in printed format again - worldwide. Most TREDITION CLASSICS titles have been out of print and off the bookstore shelves for decades. At tredition we believe that a great book never goes out of style and that its value is eternal. Several mostly non-profit literature projects provide content to tredition. To support their good work, tredition donates a portion of the proceeds from each sold copy. As a reader of a TREDITION CLASSICS book, you support our mission to save many of the amazing works of world literature from oblivion. See all available books at www.tredition.com.

Project Gutenberg

The content for this book has been graciously provided by Project Gutenberg. Project Gutenberg is a non-profit organization founded by Michael Hart in 1971 at the University of Illinois. The mission of Project Gutenberg is simple: To encourage the creation and distribution of eBooks. Project Gutenberg is the first and largest collection of public domain eBooks.

The Romance of an Old Fool

Roswell Martin Field

Imprint

This book is part of TREDITION CLASSICS

Author: Roswell Martin Field
Cover design: Buchgut, Berlin – Germany

Publisher: tredition GmbH, Hamburg - Germany
ISBN: 978-3-8472-3355-8

www.tredition.com
www.tredition.de

The intention of the TREDITION CLASSICS series is to make world literature in the public domain available in printed format. Literary enthusiasts and organizations, such as Project Gutenberg, worldwide have scanned and digitally edited the original texts. tredition has subsequently formatted and redesigned the content into a modern reading layout. Therefore, we cannot guarantee the exact reproduction of the original format of a particular historic edition. Please also note that no modifications have been made to the spelling, therefore it may differ from the orthography used today.

THE ROMANCE *of* AN OLD FOOL

I **F** it had not been for Bunsey, the novelist, I might have attained the heights. As a critic Bunsey has never commanded my highest admiration, and yet I have had my tender moments for him. From a really exacting standpoint he was not much of a novelist, and to his failure to win the wealth which is supposed to accompany fame I may have owed much of the debt of his sustained presence and his fondness for my tobacco. Bunsey had started out in life with high ideals, a resolution to lead the purely literary existence and to supply the market with a variety of choice, didactic essays along the line of high thinking; but the demand did not come up to the supply, and presently he abandoned his original lofty intention in favor of a sort of dubious romance. The financial returns, however, while a trifle more regular and encouraging, [Pg 2] were not of sufficient importance to justify him in giving up his friendly claims on my house, my library, my time, my favorite lounge, and my best brand of cigars, in return for which he contributed philosophic opinions and much strenuous advice on topics in general and literature in particular.

From my childhood I have been in the habit of keeping a diary, a running comment on the daily incidents of my pleasant but uneventful life, and occasionally, when Bunsey's society seemed too assertive and familiar, I sought to punish him by reading long and numerous excerpts. To do him justice he took the chastisement meekly, and even insisted that I was burying a remarkable talent, sometimes going to the magnanimous extreme of offering to introduce me to his publisher, and to speak a good word for me to the editors of certain magazines with whom he maintained a brisk correspondence, not infrequently of a querulous nature. All these friendly offices I gently [Pg 3] put aside, in recalling the degradation of Bunsey's ideals, though I went on tolerating Bunsey, who had a good heart and an insistent manner. In this way I possibly deprived myself of a glorious career.

My ability to befriend Bunsey was due to a felicitous chain of circumstances. When the late Mrs. Stanhope passed to her reward, she considerately left behind a document making me the recipient of her entire and not inconsiderable fortune. This proved a most unexpected blow to the church, which had enjoyed the honor and pleasure of Mrs. Stanhope's association, and which, quite naturally, had hoped to profit by her decease. The late Mrs. Stanhope, who I neglected to say was, in the eyes of Heaven, the world, and the law, my wife, had not lived with me in that utter abandonment to conjugal affection so much to be desired. We married to please our families, and we lived apart as much as possible to please ourselves. Though not without certain physical charms, Mrs. Stanhope was a [Pg 4] woman of great moral rigidity and religious austerity, who saw life through the diminishing end of a sectarian telescope, and who cared far more for the distant heathen than for the local convivial pagans who composed my *entourage*. She had brought to me a considerable sum of money, which I had increased by judicious investments, and I dare say that it was in recognition of my business ability, as well as possibly in a moment of becoming wifely remorse, that she bequeathed to me her property intact. I gave her final testimonial services wholly in keeping with her standing as a churchwoman, and I must say for my friends, whom she had severely ignored during her life, that they behaved very handsomely on that mournful occasion. They turned out in large numbers, and testified in other ways to their regard for her unblemished character. I recall, not without emotion after all these years, that Bunsey's memorial tribute to the church paper—for which he never received a [Pg 5] dollar—was a model of appreciation as well as of Christian forgiveness and self-forgetfulness.

The passing of Mrs. Stanhope made it possible for me to put into operation the long-desired plan of retiring a little way into the country, not too far from the seductions of the club and the city, but far enough to conform to the tastes of a country gentleman who likes to whistle to his dogs, putter over his roses, and meditate in a comfortable library with the poets and philosophers of his fancy. Here, with my good house-keeper, Prudence—a name I chose in preference to her mother's selection, Elizabeth—and my gardener and man of affairs, Malachy, I lived for a number of years at peace with the world and perfectly satisfied with myself. Although I was dangerously over forty, and my hair, which had been impressively dark, was conspicuously gray in spots, my figure was good, my dress correct, and my mirror told me that I was still in a position to be in the matrimonial [Pg 6] running if I tried. I mention these trifling physical details merely to save my modesty the humiliation and annoyance of referring to them in future, and to prepossess the gentle reader wherever the sex makes it highly important.

I do not deny that in certain moments of loneliness which come to us, widowers and bachelors alike, I had the impulse to tempt again the matrimonial fortune, and counting on my financial standing, together with other attractions, I ran over the eligible ladies of my acquaintance. But one was a little too old, and another was a good deal too flighty. One was too fond of society, and another did not like dogs. A fifth spoiled her chances by an unwomanly ignorance of horticulture, and a sixth perished miserably after returning to me one of my most cherished books with the leaves dog-eared and the binding cracked. For I hold with the greatest philosophers that she who maltreats a book will never make a good wife. And so the years slipped cosily [Pg 7] and cheerily by, while I grew more contented with my environment and less envious of my married friends, and whenever temporary melancholy overtook me I moved into the club for a month, or slipped across the water, finding in the change of scene immediate relief from the monotony of widowerhood.

In thus fortifying myself against the wiles of woman I was much abetted by my good Prudence, who never ceased her exhortations as to the sinister designs of her sex, and who had a ready word of discouragement for any possible candidate who might be in the line of succession. "I see that Rogers woman walkin' by the house today, Mr. John," she would begin, "and I see her turnin' her nose up at the new paint on the arbor." (I selected that color myself.) "It's queer how that woman does give herself airs, considerin' everybody knows she's been ready for ten years to take the fust man that asks her." Prudence knew that I had escorted the elderly Miss Rogers to [Pg 8] the theatre only the week before, and had commented pleasantly on the elegance of her figure. But the slight put upon my eye for color was too much. Wily Prudence!

Or a day or two after I had rendered an act of neighborly kindness to the bereaved Mrs. Stebbins she would say quite casually:

"I don't want to utter one word agin the poor and afflicted, Mr. John, but when the Widder Stebbins hit Cleo with a broom to-day I own I b'iled over. I shouldn't tell you if it warn't my duty."

Cleopatra was my favorite cocker spaniel, and any faint impression my fair neighbor may have made on my unguarded heart was immediately dispelled. Thus subtly and vigilantly my house-keeper kept the outer gates of the citadel, and shooed away a possible mistress as effectually as she dispersed the predatory hens from the garden patch.

But with the younger generation of women, good Prudence was less cautious. [Pg 9] Any maiden under the very early twenties she regarded fair material for my friendly offices, and frequently she visited me with expressions commendatory of good conduct.

"I likes to see you with the children, Mr. John, bless 'em, sir. And they do all seem to be so fond of you. There's nothin' that keeps the heart so young and fresh as goin' with young people, just as nothin' ages a man so much as havin' a lot of widders and designin' old maids about. Of course," she added, with a return of her natural suspicion, "you are old enough to be father to the whole bunch, which keeps people from talkin'."

Whether it was Prudence's approbation or my own inclination I cannot say, but it soon came about that I was on paternally familiar terms with the entire neighborhood of maidens of reasonably tender years, and a very important factor in young feminine councils. These artful creatures knew exactly when their favorite [Pg 10] roses were in bloom, exactly when the cherries back of the house were ripe, exactly when it was time to go to town for another theatre party, to give a picnic up the river, or a small and informal dance in the parlors. I was expected to remember and observe all birthdays, to be a well-spring of benevolence at Christmas, and a free and never-failing florist at Easter. I was the recipient of all young griefs and troubles, and no girl ever committed herself unconditionally to the arms of her lover until she had talked the matter over with Uncle John. All this, to a good-looking man of—well, considerably over forty, was flattering, but no sinecure.

One morning, in the late spring, it came over me unhappily that in a moment of fatal forgetfulness I had promised to be present that evening at a card-party—a promise exacted by the "Rogers woman," *persona non grata* to Prudence. A card-party was to me in the category with battle and murder and sudden death, from [Pg 11] which we all petition to be delivered in the book of common prayer—but how to be delivered? I could not be called suddenly to town, for I had already run that excuse to its full limit. I could not conveniently start for Europe on an hour's notice. The plea of sickness I dismissed as feminine and unworthy. And while I sat debating to what extreme I could tax my over-burdened conscience, Malachy appeared with the information that he had discovered unmistakable signs of cutworms in the rose-bushes, and that the local custodians of the trees were thundering against an impending epidemic of brown-tailed moth. Surely my path of duty led to the garden. But that card-party? No, let the cutworm work his will, and let the brown-tailed moth corrupt; I must take refuge in flight, however inglorious. It was then that the good angel, who never forsakes a well-meaning man, whispered to me that far back in a quiet corner of New England was the little village where I had passed my boyhood, which I had [Pg 12] deserted for five and twenty years, but which still remembered me as "Johnny" Stanhope, thanks to the officious longevity of the editor of the county paper.

The situation I explained briefly to Prudence and Malachy, and swore them into the conspiracy. I threw a few clothes into a small trunk, despatched a hypocritical note of regret to Miss Rogers, caught the noon train, and was soon beyond the danger line. Mrs. Lot, casting an apprehensive glance behind her, could not have dreaded more fearful consequences than I, looking back on the calamity I was evading. But as we went on and on into the cool, quiet country, and felt the soft air stealing down from the nearing mountains, I began to experience a lively sense of relief and pleasure, and to wonder why I had so long delayed a visit to my boyhood home.

I am sorry for the man whose childhood knew only the roar and bustle and swiftly shifting scenes of the city. For him there is no return in after years, no illusion to be [Pg 13] renewed, no joy of youth to be substantiated. His habitation has passed away or yielded to the inroads of commerce, his landmarks have vanished, and he is bewildered by the strange sights that time and trade have put upon his memories. But time has no terrors for the country-bred boy. The Almighty does not change the mountains and the rivers and the great rocks that fortify the scenery, and man is slow to push back into the far meadowlands and the hillsides, and destroy the simple, primitive life of the fathers.

All of the joy that such a returning pilgrim might have I felt when I left the train at the junction, and, scorning the pony engine and combination car supplied in later years by the railway company as a tribute to progress, set out to walk the two miles to the village. Every foot of the country I had played over as a boy. Here was the field where Deacon Skinner did his "hayin'"; just beyond the deacon raised his tobacco crop. That roof over there, [Pg 14] which I once detected as the top of Jim Pomeroy's barn, reminded me of the day of the raisin', when I sprained my ankle and thereby saved myself a thrashing for running away. Here was Pickerel Pond, the scene of many miraculous draughts, and now I crossed Peach brook which babbled along under the road just as saucily and untiringly as if it had slept all these years and was just awaking to fresh life. A hundred rods up the brook was the Widow Parsons's farm, and I knew that if I went through the side gate, cut across the barnyard, and kept down to the left, I should find that same old stump on which Bill Howland sat the day he caught the biggest dace ever pulled out of the quiet pool.

The sun was going down behind Si Thompson's planing mill as I stopped at the little red covered bridge that marked the boundary of the village. Silas had been dead for twenty years, but it seemed to me that it was only yester [Pg 15] day that I heard his nasal twang above the roar of the machinery: "Sa-ay, you fellers want to git out o' that!" The little bridge had lost much of its color and most of its impressiveness, for I remembered when to my boyish fancy it seemed a greater triumph of engineering than the Victoria bridge at Montreal. And the same old thrill went through me as I started to run—just as I did when a boy—and felt the planks loosen and creak under my feet. Here was a home-coming worth the while.

Hank Pettigrew kept the village tavern. The memory of man, so far as I knew, ran not back to the time when Hank did not keep the tavern. So I was not in the least surprised, as I entered, to see the old man, with his chair tilted back against the wall, his knees on a level with his chin, and his eyes fixed on a chromo of "Muster Day," which had descended to him through successive generations. He did not move as I advanced, or manifest the slightest emo [Pg 16] tion of surprise, merely saying, "Hullo, Johnny," as if he expected me to remark that mother had sent me over to see if he had any ice cream left over from dinner. It probably did not occur to Hank that I had been absent twenty-five years. If it had occurred to him, he would have considered such a trifling flight of time not worth mentioning.

With the question of lodging and supper disposed of, and with the modest bribe of a cigar, which Hank furtively exchanged for a more accustomed brand of valley leaf, it was not difficult to loosen the old landlord's tongue and secure information of my playmates. What had become of Teddy Grover, the pride of our school on exhibition day? Could we ever forget the afternoon he stood up before the minister and the assembled population and roared "Marco Bozzaris" until we were sure the sultan was quaking in his seraglio? And how he thundered "Blaze with your serried columns, I will not bend the knee!" To our [Pg 17] excited imaginations what dazzling triumphs the future held out for Teddy.

"Ycp; Ted's still a-beout. Three days in the week he drives stage coach over to Spicerville, and the rest o' the time he does odd jobs—sort o' tendin' round."

And Sallie Cotton—black-eyed, curly-haired, mischievous little sprite, the agony of the teacher and the love and admiration of the boys! Who climbed trees, rattled to school in the butcher wagon, never knew a lesson, but was always leading lady in the school colloquies, and was surely destined to rise to eminence on the American stage if she did not break her neck tumbling out of old Skinner's walnut tree?

"Oh, Sal; she married the Congregational minister down to Peterfield, and was 'lected president of the Temperance Union and secretary of the Endeavorers. Read a piece down at Fust Church last week on 'Breakin' Away from Old Standards,' illustratin' the alarmin' degen'racy of children nowadays."

And George Hawley, our Achilles, our [Pg 18] Samson, our ideal of everything manly and courageous! Strong as an ox and brave as a lion! Our champion in every form of athletic sports! Who looked with contempt on girls and disdained their maidenly advances! Who thought only of deeds of muscular prowess, and who seemed to carry the assurance of a force that would lead armies and subdue nations! What of George?

"Wa-al, George was a-beout not long ago. Had your room for his samples. Travellin' for a house down in Boston, and comes here reg'lar. Women folks say his last line o' shirt waists war the best they ever see."

Oh, the times that change, and change us! Alas, the fleeting years, good Posthumus, that work such havoc with our childhood dreams and hopes and aspirations!

It was a relief, after the shattering of these idols, to leave the society of the communicative Mr. Pettigrew and wander into the moonlight. Save as adding beauty to the scenery, the moon was [Pg 19] comparatively of no assistance, for so well was the little village stamped on my memory, and so little had it changed in the quarter of a century, that I could have walked blindfolded to any suggested point. Naturally I turned my steps toward the home of my youth, and as I drew near the old-fashioned, many-gabled house, with its settled, substantial air, austere yet inviting, its large yard with the huge elms, and the big lamp burning in the library or "sittin'-room," where I first dolefully studied the geography that told me of a world outside, it seemed to bend toward me rather frigidly as if to say reproachfully: "You sold me! you sold me!" True, dear old home; in my less prosperous days I was guilty of the crime of selling the house that faithfully sheltered my family for a hundred years. But have I not repented? And have I not returned to buy you back, and to make such further reparation as present conditions and true repentance demand? Is this less the pleasure than the duty of [Pg 20] wealth?

With what sensations of delight I walked softly about the grounds, taking note of every familiar tree and bush and stump. I could have sworn that not a twig, not a blade of grass, had been despoiled or had disappeared in the years that marked my absence.

I paused reverently under the old willow tree and affectionately rubbed my legs, for from this tree my parents had cut the instruments of torture for purposes of castigation, and its name, the weeping willow, was always associated in my infant mind with the direct results of contact with my unwilling person. On a level with the top of the willow was the little attic room where I slept, and the more sweetly when the crickets chirped, or the summer rain beat upon the roof, and where the song of the birds in the morning is the happiest music God has given to the country. Back of the woodshed I found the remains of an old grindstone, perhaps the same heavy crank I had so often perspiringly and reluctantly turned. Indeed [Pg 21] my reviving memories were rather too generously connected with the strenuousness and not the pleasures of youth, but I thought of the well-filled lot in the old burying-ground on the hillside, and of those lying there who had said: "My boy, I am doing this for your good." I doubted it at the time, but perhaps they were right. At all events the memories were growing pleasanter, for a stretch of thirty-five years has many healing qualities, and our childhood griefs are such little things in the afterglow.

In the early morning I renewed my rambles, going first to the little frame school-house, the old church with its tall spire, the sawmill, the deacon's cider press, the swimming pool, and a dozen other places of boyish adventure and misadventure. Your true sentimentalist invariably gives the preference to scenes over persons, and is so often rewarded by the fidelity with which they respond to his eager expectations. It was not until I had exhausted every incident of the place that I sought [Pg 22] out the companions of my school-days. What strange irony of fate is that which sends some of us out into the restless world to grow away from our old ideals and make others, and restrains some in the monotonous rut of village life, to drone peacefully their little span! But happy he, who, knowing nothing, misses nothing. If there were any village Hampdens, or mute, inglorious Miltons among my playmates, they gave no present indications. I found the girls considerably older than I expected, the boys less interesting than I hoped; but they all welcomed me with that grave, unemotional hospitality of the village, and we talked, far into the shadows, of our schooltime, the day that is never dead while memory endures.

And so it came about that at the close of day I found myself standing at the garden gate of the Eastmann cottage. Peleg Eastmann had been our village postmaster, a grave, shy man, who had received the federal office because the thrifty neighbors agreed, irrespective of political [Pg 23] feeling, that it was much less expensive to give him the office than to support him and his two daughters, the prettiest girls in our school. For they further agreed that Peleg was a "shif'less sort o' critter" and never could make a living, though he was a model postmaster and an excellent citizen and neighbor. Hence, when it came Peleg's turn to make the journey to the burying-ground in the village hearse, the whole community of Meadowvale was scandalized by the discovery that he had left his girls a comfortable little fortune, enough to keep them in modest wealth. Meadowvale never recovered from this shock. It felt that it had been victimized, and that its tenderest sensibility had been violated, and when his disconsolate daughters put up the granite shaft to their father's memory, relating that he had been faithful and just, the indignant political leader of the village remarked that it was "profanation of Scriptur'."

Thirty years ago I had stood at this little gate with one of the Eastmann [Pg 24] girls, escorting her home from Stella Perkins's party. I had attempted to kiss her good-night, and she had boxed my ears, thus contributing a disagreeable finale to an otherwise pleasant evening. Time is a great healer and I cherished no resentment at this late day toward the repudiator of my caresses. In fact I smiled in recollection of the incident as I walked up the gravelled path and knocked at the door. I wondered if the same vivacious, rosy-cheeked girl would come to meet me, and if I should feel in duty bound to make honorable amends. The door was opened by a tall, spare woman, who carried a lamp. The light reflected directly on her features, showed a face that in any other part of the world would be called hard; in New England it is merely resolute. It was the face of a woman fifty years of age, with massive chin, slightly sunken cheeks, a prominent nose, heavy eyebrows, and a high forehead rather scantily streaked by gray hair. There was no trace of the girlish bloom I had [Pg 25] known, of the beauty that once had been hers, but the imperious manner of the woman was unmistakable.

"Mary," I began jocularly, "I have come to apologize."

She thrust the lamp forward, peered into my face, and said, with not the faintest trace of a smile or the slightest evidence of embarrassment:

"Why, that's all right, Johnny Stanhope. I accept your apology. Come right in."

I went in. We sat in the sitting-room and talked of our school-days and our fortunes. I told her how I had gone down to the city, how I had prospered, of my adventures in the world, of my marriage—dealing very gently with my relations with the late Mrs. Stanhope—of my bereavement and present idyllic existence. And she told me of herself, how she had lived on and on in the little cottage, caring only for the support and education of her niece, Phyllis Kinglake, an orphan for nearly twenty years. "You [Pg 26] remember Sylvia?" she said, with the first touch of emotion.

Did I remember Sylvia? My little fair-haired playmate with the large eyes and the blue veins showing through the delicate beauty of her face? Little Sylvia, who first won my boyish affection, and with whom I made a solemn contract of marriage when we were only seven years old? Did I not remember how I would pass her house on my way to school, and stand at the gate and whistle until she came shyly out, with her face as red as her little hood and tippet, and give me her books to carry, and protest with the ever present coquetry of girlhood that she thought I had gone long ago? Could I ever forget how I saved my coppers, one by one, until I had accumulated a sum large enough to buy a whole cocoanut, which I presented to her in the proudest moment of my life, and how the other girls tossed their heads with the affectation of a sneer, and with pretended indifference to this astonishing stroke of [Pg 27] fortune? And that fatal evening when I provoked my little beauty's wrath, and in all the receding opportunities of "Post-Office" and "Copenhagen" she had turned her face and rosy lips away from me, until the world was black with a hopeless despair? And the singing-school where she was our shining ornament, and that blissful night when I stood up with her in the village church, while we sang our duet descriptive of the special virtues of some particular flower nominated in the cantata? And how, growing older and shyer, we still preserved our youthful fancy even to the day I struck out into the world, both believing in the endurance of the tie that would draw me back? What caprice of fate is it that dispels the illusions of youth and restores them tenfold in the reflection of after years and over the gulf of the grave? Did I remember Sylvia?

Then Mary went on to tell me of Sylvia's happy marriage to George Kinglake, how, when little Phyllis had come, [Pg 28] and the world was at its brightest, the parents had been stricken down in the same week by a virulent disease, and how, with her dying breath, the mother had asked her sister to look after her little one and protect her from sorrow and harm. Very simply this stern-featured woman told the story of her efforts to do her duty to her sister's child, and it seemed to me that her face grew softer and her voice gentler as she went over the years they had grown older together, while the beauty of this woman's life was glorified by the willing sacrifices of imposed motherhood. I could not see Phyllis, for she was spending the night with friends in another part of the village. Next time, she hoped, I might be more successful.

Walking slowly to the tavern my mind still went back to my little playmate and the golden days of youth, and if my heart grew a little tenderer, and my eyes were moistened by the recall, what need to be ashamed of the emotion? And if [Pg 29] in the night I dreamed that I was a boy again, and that a fair-haired child played with me in the changing glow of dreamland in the best and purest scenes of the human comedy, was it a delusion to be dispelled, a memory to be put aside? Did I remember Sylvia?

[Pg 30]

T **HE** thought that my train was to [Pg 31] leave at ten o'clock did not depress me as I awoke, with the sunlight streaming through the window, for, after all, I was obliged to admit that the monotony of Meadowvale and the sluggishness of my village friends were beginning to have an appreciable effect. Then the memory of little Sylvia came to me again, and nothing seemed pleasanter, as a benediction to the old days, than a visit to the burying-ground where she was sleeping. The previous day I had paid the obligations of remembrance and respect to the graves of my kindred, and it gave me at first an uncomfortable feeling to realize that the thought of them was less potent than the recollection of this young girl. But was it strange or inexcusable? Had they not lived out their lives of honored usefulness, and grown old and weary of the battle? And had not she passed away just as the greater joys of living were unfolding, [Pg 32] and the assurance of happiness was the stronger? Poor Sylvia!

The spectacle of a correctly dressed, middle-aged man passing down the street, bearing a somewhat cumbersome burden of lilies-of-the-valley and forget-me-nots, must have had its peculiar significance to the inhabitants of the village, and many curious glances were my reward. I passed along, however, without explanations in distinct violation of rural etiquette. The old caretaker of the burying-ground met me at the entrance and gave me the directions—second path to the right, half way up the hill, just to the left of the big elm. The old man had known me as a boy and would have detained me in conversation, but I pleaded that my time was short, and reluctantly he let me go my way. Slowly up the hill I walked, occasionally pausing to place a forget-me-not on the grave of one I had known in childhood. Even old Barrows did not escape my passing tribute—a cynical, cross-grained old [Pg 33] fellow, the aversion of the boys, who tormented him and whom he tormented with reciprocal vigor. No need of a forget-me-not for Barrows, for he never forgot anything, so I gave his somewhat neglected grave the token of a long stem of little lilies, in evidence that the past was forgiven, and moved on to avoid possible protestation.

I paused under the wide-branching elm to recover my breath. The assent had been arduous for a gentleman inclined to portliness and with wind impaired by tobacco. I turned to the left, and at that moment, just before me, a woman's figure slowly rose from the ground. A creeping sensation possessed me. My heart bounded and my pulses thrilled. Was this Sylvia risen from the dead? Surely it was Sylvia's graceful girlish form! This was Sylvia's oval face, with Sylvia's large gray eyes. In such a way Sylvia's pretty light hair waved about her temples, and the pink and white of her delicate complexion revealed the [Pg 34] blue veins. Twenty-five years had rolled back in an instant, and I was standing in the presence of the past. Alas, the swift passing of the illusion, for the conversation of the evening came to me.

"You are Phyllis?" I said.

"I am Phyllis," she answered softly—her mother's voice—"and you are Mr. Stanhope. My aunt told me."

I did not answer, for I was staring stupidly at her, reluctant to abandon the pleasing fancy that my thinking of her had brought her back from the dead again. She did not speak, but glanced inquiringly at the flowers I held in my hand.

"I knew your mother, Phyllis," I managed to say. "She was a very dear playmate of my childhood. I have brought these flowers to put upon her grave. Shall we go together?"

The girl's eyes filled, and she pointed to the rising mound at her feet. Silently we bent over and reverently laid the lilies and forget-me-nots under the simple [Pg 35] headstone.

"May I talk to you of your mother?" I asked.

We sat down on a rude bench in the path, and I told her of my childhood, of the days when Sylvia and I were sweethearts, of our little quarrels and frolics, of her mother's beauty and gentleness. The girl laughed at the recital of our misadventures, and the tears came into her eyes when I touched on my boyish affection for my playmate. Then she told me of her own life, so peaceful and happy in the little village, and in the neighboring town, where she had been educated with all the care and diligence of the New England impulse. I looked at my watch.

"It is quarter past eleven," I said ruefully, "and my train left at ten."

"There's another train at three," she replied. "You will go home and dine with us? We dine at twelve in the country, you know."

If I was somewhat ashamed to face [Pg 36] Mary Eastmann, she received us with the same stolidity she had manifested when we first met, and at once insisted that I should remain for dinner. "Go into the parlor," she said abruptly.

Phyllis plucked the sleeve of my coat. "Don't go in there," she whispered; "that's Aunt Mary's room exclusively, and I'm afraid you'll not find it very cheerful. Come out on the porch."

"I know the room," I whispered back, as we went out together. "At least I know the type. Lots of horse-hair belongings. Square piano against the wall. Wax flowers under a glass case on the mantel. Steel engravings of Washington crossing the Delaware. Family album, huge Bible, and 'Famous Women of Two Centuries' on the centre table. Seashells, blue wedgwood and German china things mingled in delightful confusion on the what-not. If not wax flowers, it's wax fruit."

Phyllis laughed—how much her laugh was like her mother's—and nodded her [Pg 37] head. "Not a bad description," she assented; "you must have the gift of second sight."

"Not second sight. Suppose we call it the gift of second childhood."

We sat on the porch and looked down on the lawn that sloped to the orchard, and watched the robins run across the grass. And I pointed out to Phyllis the very tree under which Sylvia and I had stood the day we had our first memorable quarrel, confessing that while at the time there was no doubt in my mind that Sylvia was clearly at fault, I was now prepared to concede, after plenty of reflection, that possibly she might have had a reasonable defence. The recital of this pathetic incident led to other reminiscences connected with the old house and its grounds, and I was hardly in the second chapter when Mary came out and ordered us in to dinner. Mary never invited, never requested; she merely ordered. We sat at the table, and at a severe look from Mary I stopped fumbling with my [Pg 38] napkin, while Phyllis—sweet saint!—folded her hands and asked the divine blessing. Pagan philosopher that I was, I was singularly moved by the simple faith of these two women, and I think that when I am led back into the fold of my family creed, a girl as young and fair and holy as Phyllis will be the angel to guide me.

The dinner was toothsome, the environment fascinating, the afternoon perfect, and so it came about quite naturally that I missed the three-o'clock train. "There is nothing so disagreeable in life," I explained apologetically to my friends, "as a hard and fast schedule, which keeps one jumping like an electric clock, doing sixty things every hour and never varying the performance. Fortunately trains run every day except Sunday, and the general order of the universe is not going to be upset because I am not checking myself off like a section-hand."

Perhaps Mary did not wholly coincide with my argument, but she was called [Pg 39] away to her sewing-circle, while Phyllis and I lounged lazily on the porch, I continuing my reminiscences. Garrulity is not merely the prerogative of age; the privilege of the monologue is always that of the old boy who comes back to his childhood's home and finds in a pretty girl a charming and attentive listener. He is a poor orator, indeed, who cannot improve such opportunities. At a convenient lull in the flow of discourse we went off to ride, exploring the country roads I knew so well, and here began new matter and new reminiscences, patiently endured by Phyllis, who was a most delightful girl. And when we returned late in the afternoon it was directly in the line of circumstances that I should remain for tea; and after tea Phyllis played and sang for me in the little parlor, for Phyllis was a musician of no small merit. When in reply to my inquiry she sang a simple Scotch ballad her mother had sung so touchingly many years before, a great lump rose in my throat, and I sat far over [Pg 40] in the shadow that she and Mary might not see how blurred were my eyes, and how unmanageable my emotion. At what age does it come to a man and a philosopher that he is no longer ashamed of honest, sympathetic tears?

I shall never know whether it was the journey in the train, the air and cooking of Meadowvale, or the visits to the burying-ground, that upset me, but for the first time in a dozen years I found myself dissatisfied with my home. I remarked to Malachy that the roses seemed to be in a most discouraging condition, and that the garden in general was altogether disappointing. I noticed that my dogs barked a great deal, that the neighbors had become most tiresome, and that Bunsey was an unmitigated nuisance. Even the cuisine, which had been my pride and boast, grew at times unbearable, and I had not been home a fortnight before I astonished Prudence by positively assuring her that the dinner she had set before me was not worth any [Pg 41] sane man's serious attention. Whereupon that excellent woman announced with superb pride that she "guessed it was about time for that Rogers woman to give another card-party."

"Prudence," I said severely, for I encourage no flippancy on the part of domestics, "that remark, while probably hasty and ill-considered, borders on impertinence. I shall overlook it this time on account of your faithful services in the past. But don't let it happen again. In any event," I amended considerately, "don't let it drop in my presence."

Thinking it over I came to the conclusion that Prudence was right in the general effect of the suggestion. What I needed was a change of scene. Long abstention from travel and variety of incident had made me restless and discontented. I had not been in Europe for two years. Undoubtedly I was pining for a lazy tour of the Continent. The thought decided me. I should book my passage on the steamer that sailed the [Pg 42] Saturday of the following week.

Strangely enough, at this interesting moment, I received a letter from the chairman of the committee on public improvements in the village of Meadowvale, announcing that it had been resolved to procure new rooms for the village library, and would Mr. John Stanhope do his native village the honor of subscribing a small amount toward this desirable end. As it is always much easier for an indolent man to telegraph than to write letters, I replied by wire that Mr. Stanhope felt himself much honored by the request. Not entirely satisfied with this confession, I sent a second telegram an hour later doubling my subscription. Still my conscience troubled me.

"I have not done my duty," I said to myself. "Here I am, a man of means, I may say of large wealth, with no special obligations resting upon me, and yet I have done nothing to benefit or enrich my old home. It is strange that it has not occurred to me before what a privilege, [Pg 43] what an honor, it is to be a philanthropist even in a small way, and with what alacrity those whom Heaven has blessed with a fortune should respond to the calls of deserving need. I blush for my past thoughtlessness, and I shall hasten to atone for my astonishing neglect. My duty lies before me, and I shall not shrink from it, whatever the personal inconvenience."

Thereupon I telegraphed for the third time to the chairman that it would give Mr. Stanhope the greatest pleasure to put up a suitable library for the village of Meadowvale, and, in order to guard against any possible misunderstanding, he would depart the following day to confer with the committee as to site and probable extent of the structure. This concession to my conscience comforted me greatly, and I prepared for my journey with a lightness that was almost buoyancy. The chairman and two of the committee met me at the junction. They were most deprecatory and apologetic, [Pg 44] and mentioned with evident sorrow the absence of several of the members which might cause a postponement of the conference until the following day. I bore up under this intelligence with astonishing cheerfulness.

"My good friends," I said, "don't let this disturb you for a minute. I am not so pressed for time that I cannot wait on your reasonable convenience. Your tavern is well kept and the food is wholesome. I think I may say that my old friends in Meadowvale will interest me until we can come to an amicable understanding. Suppose, to be sure of a full meeting, that we fix the time of conference at day after to-morrow—a little late in the afternoon."

After this suggestion had been received with suitable expressions of gratitude, we journeyed together to the village, where I was duly turned over to old Pettigrew. And then, as the day was by no means done, I strolled down the street and, most naturally and quite unthinkingly, [Pg 45] found myself a few minutes later looking over the Eastmann gate at Phyllis on the porch. To say that this charming girl was surprised by my sudden appearance was no less true than to admit that she did not seem in the least displeased. I positively had no intention of going in, but before I knew it I was sitting beside her, relating in the most casual way the reason of my coming.

"How good it was of you," said the ingenuous creature, "and how delighted and grateful Meadowvale will be. It must be glorious to be rich enough to do things for other people."

Now it is not a disagreeable sensation to feel that one is rich and good and glorious in the large gray eyes of a very pretty woman, and I was conscious of the mild intoxication from the compliment. "It is, indeed," I answered magnanimously. "I have always maintained that money is given to us in trust for those around us, and that in making others happy we find our greatest happiness. [Pg 46]

I regret that I have not wholly lived up to this undeniably correct principle."

"It will require at least a thousand dollars," she said naïvely.

"Oh, at least."

She was silent a moment. Then she said: "I was wondering what I would do if I had a thousand dollars to give away."

"What do you think you would do?"

"Speaking for my own preferences I think I should like to establish a country club."

"The very thing. If there is one crying want more than another in Meadowvale it is a country club, with golf links, tennis courts, and shower baths."

"Now you are laughing at me."

"Not at all. Fancy old Hank and you playing a foursome with Aunt Mary and me for the cider and apples. Why, it would add years of robustness to our waning lives."

"No," said the girl decisively. "It [Pg 47] isn't feasible."

"Then," I went on musingly, "we might have an Art Institute, or the Phyllis Kinglake School of Expression, or the Meadowvale Woman's Club, or the Colonial Dames, or, best of all, the Daughters of the American Revolution."

"That shows how little you appreciate the local situation," she responded quickly, "for your best of all is worse and worse. Imagine an order of Daughters in a place where every woman's ancestors did nothing but fight in the Revolution. As well call a town meeting at once. Ah,"—with a sigh—"I see that I shall never spend the thousand dollars in Meadowvale."

"Don't be too sure of that, my dear Phyllis," I exclaimed in an outburst, for I was in a particularly happy and generous mood; "and remember that when you do decide how the money is to be philanthropically invested we shall see that it is forthcoming."

With such agreeable banter the minutes [Pg 48] slipped away, and when Mary appeared with the customary invitation to tea, it would have been a jolt to the harmonious order of things to decline. I cannot say that I have ever cordially approved the austerity of the New England tea-table, with its cold bread and biscuits, its applesauce, its frugal allowance of sardines, its basket of cake, and its not very stimulating pot of tea. But such are the compensations of pleasant society that even these chilly viands may be forgotten, and I said my "Amen" to Phyllis's sweet and modest grace with all the heartiness of a thankful man. As no gentleman may, with propriety, run away immediately after he has accepted hospitality, I lingered in the evening, and we had more music, which so calmed and rested me that I wondered at my past nervousness and marvelled that I had even contemplated a journey across the water.

How it came about that the next morning Phyllis and I were strolling over the village, down by the river and into the [Pg 49] pleasant woods, I have forgotten, but I dare say that we were discussing further developments of philanthropy, and endeavoring to come to a conclusion as to the proper disposition of that troublesome thousand dollars. The girl was so young and joyous, so pretty, so arch, so fascinating with that little coquettishness that is not the usual type of the Puritan maiden, I could not find it in my heart to remember Mary's words and "try to instil in her a closer appreciation of the more serious purposes of life." Indeed life is so serious that it is one of the blessed decrees of Mother Nature that we have that brief allotment of time when it is too serious to think about, and youth passes so quickly that it is criminal to rob it of its golden hour. In such a presence I felt my own spirits rising, my step becoming springy, my whole nature less sluggish, and, had I looked in the mirror, I should have confidently expected to see a youthful bloom in my cheeks and a return of [Pg 50] hair to primary conditions.

It is due to this interesting young woman to say that she coyly urged me not to forget my other friends, since I was to leave so soon, and it pleased me to fancy that she was not altogether offended when I spoke somewhat hastily and rather flippantly of those of my former companions who had lapsed into tediousness. I reminded her also that as the happiest memory of my childhood was associated with her mother, so it was sweet to me to be with her and live again, in a pleasant dream, the brightness of the past. Then, for her mother's sake, she shyly let me take her hand while I went over again, not without emotion, the story of my early love. Dear little Sylvia!

The meeting of the committee was followed by a general congregation of citizens, and I was invited to the platform, where I outlined my plans. I hinted that the library was merely the beginning of a number of beneficences which I desired to contribute to Meadowvale's prosperity, [Pg 51] and as I looked down upon my listeners and caught sight of Phyllis, glancing up with flushed cheeks and sparkling eyes, I was nearly betrayed into promises of the most preposterous nature. At the end of my remarks—I recall that I spoke with unusual grace and eloquence—the chairman stood up and gravely thanked me, intimating that I was a credit to Meadowvale and its perfect public school system. I fancy I should have been applauded if it had been compatible with the nature of the people of Meadowvale to make so riotous a demonstration. At the close of the meeting it happened, by the purest accident, that I walked home with Mary and Phyllis, and when Mary said in her blunt way that I really had been most generous, Phyllis did not speak, but she slipped her hand under my arm and gave me an appreciative little squeeze, which made me regret that I had not pledged another thousand.

I was to leave the next morning, thanks [Pg 52] to the officious members of the committee, who had so blunderingly hurried matters to accommodate me that I had no longer an excuse of remaining. And it was for this reason that I went in and sat again in the little parlor, while Phyllis sang for me the songs that were my favorites, and some her mother sang in the long ago. Memories were again pleasantly stirred within me, as was not infrequent in those days, and I experienced all the happiness that comes to him who is persuaded that he has made himself a little above the ordinary attractions of the earth. In this excess of good feeling, and stimulated alike by the music and the consciousness of a philanthropic impulse, I waited until the moment of parting before declaring definitely my excellent intentions.

"My dear Mary," I began, turning to that admirable spinster, "you know how our childhood was linked by a close family feeling, and how you and Sylvia and I planned in our simple ambitions to live

[Pg 53] together in the great world outside. We may say now that this was childish romance, and that the caprice of time has made it an idle fancy. For many years we have been separated, and only by a happy chance have we been brought together. Fortune has been kind to me. I am called a rich man, and I believe I may say without boasting that I am far beyond the need of anxiety. But to a degree I am a lonely man. My sister's child is my one near relative in the world, and he is a young man with an excellent business, able to take care of himself, and naturally engrossed with his own occupations. You can understand that at my time of life, alone as I am, and still young enough to appreciate the joys of living, I have a feeling of desolation for which no riches can compensate. Had fortune given me a daughter, like our Phyllis here, I think no happiness could have been so great. It has pleased me to look back upon the past, to recall the days of our childhood, and to see in [Pg 54] Phyllis the image of her mother. Why can I not link the present and the future with the past? Why can I not look on Phyllis as my own daughter, and give to her all the father love I have learned to feel? I do not rob you either of her love or her presence. I merely add a new joy to my life, and know that in caring for you both and in contributing to her happiness, and securing her against misfortune after we are taken away, I am carrying out the pledge, however idle at the time, I made to Sylvia."

I fancied I saw what may have been the suspicion of a tear in Mary Eastmann's eye. It vanished as quickly as it came, and when she spoke and thanked me for my generous offer, her voice was as calm and her manner as collected as if I had made a casual suggestion for attendance at a prayer meeting. She could not deny that the opportunity was too enticing to be ignored, and she admitted that my fatherly proposition was distinctly advantageous. Her New England [Pg 55] independence rather revolted at the thought of any immediate financial assistance, which was not needed, while her New England thrift approved a future settlement based on family friendliness of many years' standing. On the whole she was inclined to be favorable to my point of view.

As for Phyllis, she had listened to me with undisguised amazement. Her big gray eyes had grown larger, and the color left her cheeks as I finished. Then the rosy red rushed back, her lip quivered and the tears sprang to her eyes. A moment later she smiled, then laughed, and was serious again. How incomprehensible are these young girls! Poor child! she had never known a father's love.

Phyllis followed me to the door. The light, streaming from the parlor, shone squarely on her exquisite face. A thrill of pleasure went through me as I realized that at last I had a daughter whom I could love and cherish. I took her [Pg 56] hand in both of mine, and, as I released it, I parted the light, wavy hair, and kissed her forehead. It seemed to me that she trembled slightly, but in a moment she was herself, and a gleam of merriment was in her eyes, as she said:

"Of course you will write to me—papa?"

Doubtless the novelty of the situation made me just a little embarrassed. To be called "papa" the first time by a pretty girl was more embarrassing than I had expected. And why that half-laugh in her eye, and why that almost quizzical tone? Was I not kind and good enough to be her father, and had I not tried to show her every paternal consideration? Was I not honestly endeavoring to fulfil a sacred pledge? I was perplexed but not discouraged. "I will prove to her," I said to myself with firmness, "that I am entirely worthy of her filial affection, and that she may lean confidently upon me." And I went [Pg 57] straightway to bed, and dreamed of her all night as every true father should dream of the daughter of his heart and his hope.

[Pg 58]

I **N** the very nature of things it was [Pg 59] necessary that I should return frequently to Meadowvale, to confer with the village committee and make all proper arrangements for beginning so important a local enterprise. While this put an end to my projected trip to Europe I accepted the situation with calmness and forbearance, satisfied that in the pursuit of duty and in giving happiness to my fellow creatures I should have the reward of an approving conscience. To my nephew, Frederick Grinnell, I gave the task of preparing the plans, and his excellent suggestions were cordially adopted. Much of my spare time—and it is amazing how much spare time one has in a village—was spent at the Eastmann cottage with my new daughter, and in the evening I talked to her of the world outside, quite, I fancy, as Othello may have spoken to Desdemona, but with a more conservative and a better impulse. I unfolded [Pg 60] to her the wonders of great London, the pleasures of Paris, the beauties of Venice, the sacred mysteries of Rome, the noble traditions of Athens. I journeyed with her up the Nile and down the Rhine. One night we were in gay Vienna, another in Berlin, a third in the grandeur of the Alhambra. From the fjords of Norway to the tea houses of Japan was the journey of a few minutes, and the indifference of my surfeited life gave way before the kindling enthusiasm of this lovely country girl, whose world had been the area of scarcely more than a township.

But the paternal relation, however honest and commendable my intentions, did not seem to thrive as I had fondly hoped. Only in her teasing moments would this vivacious creature admit the solemnity of our compact, and when she called me "papa" there was always that gleam of the eye, with that merriment of tone, which may not have been disrespectful but was certainly not filial. [Pg 61] This troubled me exceedingly. I thought it all over and one night I said to her:

"My dear Phyllis, it has become only too evident that you do not entertain that deferential feeling for me which a daughter should have for a father. I shall not describe your emotions as I have analyzed them, but I am satisfied that we shall not make a complete success of my long cherished plan. However, I am not prepared to withdraw unreservedly from my schemes for your comfort and happiness, and since you cannot look upon me as a father, or treat me like a father, I have another suggestion to offer. Let me be your elder brother, and watch over and guard you as a brother's duty should direct. There shall be no diminution of my love, no retraction of my promises. Perhaps, in the feeling that I am your brother, you will talk with me with greater frankness, and feel more closely drawn to me, and we shall be all the better and the happier for the change."

Thus speaking I took her pretty hand [Pg 62] and carried it respectfully to my lips, at the same time patting it affectionately and assuring her of my brotherly devotion. And this incomprehensible girl threw back her head and laughed; then burst into tears, laughed again, flushed to crimson and ran out of the room. I was grieved beyond measure. Had I done wrong so quickly and rudely to sever a connection so holy? Had the filial feeling been suddenly awakened in her breast? Was I depriving this poor child of a tender paternal care, for which she longed, but which maidenly coyness could not immediately accept?

As a philosopher I have made woman the subject of much research, and my library bears witness to the attention I have paid to the written opinions of the ablest writers and thinkers of all times, who have had anything to do with this fascinating theme. I have seen her in all her phases, analyzed her in all her emotions, and Bunsey has admitted to me that my theoretical knowledge has been [Pg 63] of great value to him in dealing subtly with his heroines. And yet, despite my complete equipment in mental construction, I am constantly surprised by a new development, a sudden and unaccountable phenomenon of feminine nature, which undoubtedly escaped the experience and reasoning of the experts and sages. It is indeed a matter of pride in woman that while man has studied her for thousands of years, she continues to exhibit fresh delights in her infinite variety of moods and to put forth unexpectedly new and astounding shoots.

I saw Phyllis no more that evening, save in my dreams, and it was wholly creditable to the goodness of my motives and the sincerity of my affection that she abided with me in my slumbering fancies with no protracted intermissions. The next day she was as sweet and gracious as ever, but I thought her tone a little constrained, and when, as a father or brother should, I ventured to speak of the tenderness of our family relation, a half-imploring look came into her beautiful eyes. And [Pg 64] when I casually remarked on the softness of her hair, or the slenderness of her fingers, her glance was timidly reproachful. All this gave me great unhappiness, and I discovered, to my further distress, that in my attempt to return to the old familiar footing I was neglecting the committee and losing interest in the affairs of the library. A certain peevishness took possession of me; I was no longer myself, and I lost the gayety and sprightliness which had been always my distinguishing virtues.

Furthermore I missed the companionship and solace of my books in this emergency, for I had no reference library to which I could go in Meadowvale for aid in establishing the true condition of this strange girl. I recalled dimly that somewhere on my shelves was a volume which contained a fairly analogous case, but while I knew that I possessed such a book I could not remember the circumstances or the incidents cited, and this added to my unrest. Only a student can understand [Pg 65] the absolute wretchedness which overtakes a man when he finds himself miserably dependent on a distant library. For several days I gave myself up entirely to my mental depression, greatly wondering at the perplexing change in my life, and marvelling that in all my explorations in philosophy I had not provided for just such a crisis, whatever it might be. One afternoon as I sat in my room at the tavern, looking idly out of the window and across the little river which rippled by, something seemed to strike me violently in the forehead. It may have been a telepathic suggestion, it may have been a return to consciousness; at all events it was an idea. I leaped from my chair, put on my hat, and proceeded rather feverishly to the Eastmann cottage. Phyllis was away for the day; Mary was knitting in the sitting-room. I watched her in silence for a moment, and then I said abruptly:

"Mary, I think I should like to marry Phyllis."

Mary Eastmann was not the type of [Pg 66] woman to lose herself or betray astonishment. She pushed her spectacles sharply above her eyes, looked at me sternly, and said in a rasping voice.

"John Stanhope, don't be an old fool."

"Whatever I may be, Mary," I answered, much nettled by her tone, "I do not think anybody can properly regard me as a fool. As for the other qualification," I went on complacently, "I am not so old."

"You and Sylvia were the same age, and she would have been forty-eight."

"A man is as old as he feels," I ventured, finding refuge in a proverb.

"That is evasive, and has nothing to do with the question. Beside, what reason have you to believe that Phyllis has the slightest desire to marry you?"

"Frankly, not the slightest reason in the world," I replied with the utmost candor. "That is why I have been so bold as to speak to you on the subject."

"Perhaps you thought I might use my influence to help you along?"

"Quite the contrary, my dear Mary, I [Pg 67] assure you. I may not know very much about women"—I was quite humble when separated from my library—"but I do know that nothing is so fatal to a lover's prospects as the encouragement of the loved one's relations. You see that I am perfectly frank."

"Then you wish my opposition?"

"Come, let us be reasonable. I have told you I wish to marry Phyllis. I know my good points, and I am not unacquainted with my weak ones. Unhappily I can figure out my age to a day. Alas, I am forty-eight, and Phyllis is not yet twenty-three. The difference is positively ghastly from a sentimental standpoint, but if I love her, and she is not hopelessly indifferent to me, I think that even that difficulty can be bridged. You know my position, my character, my general reputation. Neither of us knows what Phyllis really thinks or what she will say or do in the matter. I do not ask either for your opposition or your good offices. I have come to you as an old friend and the girl's [Pg 68] nearest relative to tell you exactly how I feel and what I wish to gain. And I ask only that I may have the same chance to win her affection that you might grant to a younger man."

Mary's voice was gentler when she spoke again. "John," she said, "Phyllis is all I have in the world. It is my one idea to have her happily married to a worthy man whom she honestly loves. Providence, in inscrutable wisdom, may have decreed that you are that man, but," she continued with a sudden return of Yankee caution, "I have my doubts, considering your age. However, you have acted honorably in coming to me, and while I think Phyllis would be a better daughter than wife to you, I cannot speak for her. Remember that she is very young and very inexperienced. Her acquaintance with men has been slight. You are a man of the world and with enough of the surface polish—I don't say it stops with that—to dazzle any girl accustomed to such surroundings as we have here. [Pg 69] Undoubtedly an offer from you would flatter her; it might induce her to accept you, thinking that she loved you. Be careful. Be sure of your ground before it is too late."

As I walked back to the village I mused on what Mary had said, but I felt no apprehension. Most lovers are alike in this—in youth, in middle age, in senility. Perhaps the advantage of middle life is that a man is more the master of himself, more in possession of the faculties necessary to carry him through a crisis. Without the impetuous desire of youth, or the deadened sensibilities of old age, he has a certain serene confidence that is a mixture of love and philosophy. It disturbed me somewhat to find with what equanimity I faced a situation which promised nothing. It really annoyed me to note that I was picking out mentally the place to which I should conduct Phyllis in order to have the harmonious environment adapted to a sentimental proposition. I remembered that down by the river, [Pg 70] just beyond the willows, there was an old tree where Sylvia and I—ah, so many years ago!—had sat and talked of our lives before us. To that sacred spot I would lead Sylvia's daughter, and, passing gently from the past to the present, I would tell her of my love and of my fondest hopes. How dignified and appropriate such a spot for a frank, calm, and self-contained avowal!

Thus philosophically and amiably plotting I walked contentedly along, and, looking up, I saw Phyllis coming toward me, swinging her hat in her hand, and suggesting in her girlish beauty and graceful outline the poet's shepherdess. She did not see me, and, yielding to a sudden impulse, I stepped quickly aside in the shadow of a neighbor's house, as she passed on with her eyes on the ground. I followed at a little distance, and discovered, much to my dismay, that she chose the road that led to the burying-ground. Now a cemetery is not at all the spot that a man, whatever his philosophy, would select for a tender [Pg 71] declaration, but I was buoyed by the remembrance of Mary's words. "The finger of Providence may be in it," I muttered. "The Lord's will be done."

Slowly up the winding path she walked, and I as slowly followed. When I reached her, she was standing at her mother's grave, just as she had stood the morning we first met. I tried to accept this as an omen, but failed miserably, and omens, after all, depend on the point of view. She raised her eyes, and, seeing me, blushed, another omen which means comparatively little to a man who is aware of the thousand emotions that are responsible for the blush of woman. I was again annoyed by the discovery that my pulses were not beating wildly, and that my heart was not throbbing tumultuously, and when I addressed a commonplace remark to her I was thoroughly ashamed and humiliated. It seemed like taking a mean advantage of innocence and inexperience.

We sat together on the little bench, and for the first time in our acquaintance [Pg 72] she appeared embarrassed, as if she knew what was passing in my mind. I have always believed that women, in addition to their acknowledged intuition, have a special sense that enables them to anticipate a declaration of passion, and I had no doubt that Phyllis was fully prepared for my confession in spite of her embarrassment. This induced me to proceed to the point without unnecessary preliminaries.

"Phyllis," I said, not without a certain agreeable ardor, "I have been talking with Aunt Mary."

"Indeed?"

"And about you."

"Really?"

"When I say that I have been talking with Aunt Mary, and about you," I continued in a grieved tone, for I do not like jerky responses, "I wish you to understand that it was in connection with no ordinary topic. Phyllis,"—I spoke with the utmost tenderness—"can you not guess the nature of our discussion?"

Phyllis was equal to the emergency; [Pg 73] her embarrassment had disappeared. "I am glad," she said, "that your conversation so far as it related to me was out of the ordinary. I suppose I may ask what the topic was—that is, if you don't mind telling."

This was approaching the serious. "Phyllis, I was telling Aunt Mary that I loved you and wished to make you my wife."

A flash, half merry, half angry, came to her eye. "That was thoughtful of you. Is it customary for gentlemen in the city, when they think they love a girl, to honor all her relations with their confidence before they speak to the girl herself?"

I took her hand. She made the slightest motion to withdraw it, and permitted it to remain in my grasp. "Phyllis," I said with all earnestness, "do not misunderstand me. I sought you at the house. You were absent. Your Aunt Mary and I have been friends from childhood, and it was only natural that out of my heart I spoke the words that were in [Pg 74] my mind. I told her that I loved you, just as at that moment I might have shouted it from the housetop. My heart was full of you and I had to speak. Can't you understand?"

The girl was still obdurate, and she spoke with some petulance. "If that is the case, perhaps it is just as well that it was Aunt Mary and not one of the neighbors."

"Dear little Phyllis, you are not angry with me because I love you? You cannot remain angry with me because I confessed my love before I met you to-day? If you had only seen with what applications of cold water your aunt rewarded my confidence, you would pity and not reproach me."

For a minute the girl was silent. Then she asked softly: "How long have you known that you loved me?"

"Must I answer that question candidly and unreservedly?"

"Unreservedly and candidly."

I seized her other hand and held her [Pg 75] firmly. "About fifty minutes."

She laughed, rather joyously I thought. "And having loved me for fully fifty minutes, you wish to make me your wife? Confiding man!"

"Little girl," I said tenderly, "let us be serious. If my dull consciousness did not awaken till an hour ago, my heart tells me that I have loved you ever since I first saw you standing near this spot. I am not going to ask you now whether you love me, or ever can learn to love me. It is happiness enough for me to-day to know how much I love you, and to know that I have told you of that love. I do not care to have my dream too rudely and too suddenly dispelled. Very probably you do not care for me as I should like to have you care for me, but do not make a jest of my affection. I am wholly aware of the preposterousness of my demands in many respects"—this sounded very conventional and commonplace, but every lover must say it—"and, believe me, I shudder when I think of what I have dared confess." [Pg 76]

Then she said with the most delightful demureness: "Mr. Stanhope, is it likely that a girl would sit in a burying-ground on a bench with a gentleman, allowing him to hold both her hands, unless she cared for him a little—just a little?"

Up to this moment I had fairly forgotten that I was depriving her of all power of resistance, but with such encouragement I took an even more sympathetic grasp and sat a trifle closer, while the minutes ticked away. A robin flew down from the tree near by and saucily hopped toward us, until at a rebuking call from his mate he flew away, and I fancied that I could hear them talking over the situation, and drawing conclusions from their own happiness. Phyllis was the first to break the charming spell.

"Mr. Stanhope," she asked, hardly above a whisper, "what did Aunt Mary say when you told her that you wished to make me your wife?"

"She said, Phyllis, that Providence may [Pg 77] have decreed that I am the man to bring you happiness."

And still in that same enchanting whisper, with her face a little rosier, as she half hid it below my shoulder: "Mr. Stanhope, do you think that a girl with my Christian training could fly in the face of Providence?"

[Pg 78]

T **HE** philosopher was in love. It [Pg 79] comes, I have no doubt, to every well-ordered man to be in love once. Some there are who maintain, with plausibility, that the passion we call love may be of frequent recurrence, and they point to the passing fancies of boys and girls, the romances of moonlight, the repeated sighings of the fickle Corydon, and the matrimonial entanglements of the aging Lydia, as evidence for their argument. That there are varying degrees of the ecstatic emotion cannot be truthfully denied. Heaven has wisely decreed that the heart, once filled with its ideal, may be compensated for the bitter hour of sorrow by the soothing balm of a new affection, and it is even possible that the second love may be more satisfying than the first, the third or fourth more typical of exaltation than its predecessors. But love, whether early or late, in the perfect absorption of the faculties comes only once; as compared with this remarkable mental state all other [Pg 80] conditions are unemotional, unfilling.

The true lover rises early, before the world is astir. If it is summer and in the country, his thoughts lead him to the cool groves, the shady banks of the river, the retired spots where he may uninterruptedly commune with his happiness or his misery, and reflect on the blessings that are to be, or should be, his. Was it not then as a true lover that in the early morning I walked into the country, and down the banks of the stream where Sylvia and I had strayed and talked in the sunny days of youth? And nature seemed a part of the wedding procession, and the squirrels on the fence rails, and the robins, wrens, and wood-thrushes in the trees chirped and twittered: "John Stanhope is in love! John Stanhope is in love!" And the mocking crow, lazily flapping his wings at a safe distance, croaked enviously: "Ha, ha! old Stanhope is in love. Ha, ha!" Yet the whole conspiracy of animated nature could not make old Stanhope in his present exaltation regretful of [Pg 81] his age or ashamed of his passion.

Mary Eastmann had accepted the situation without comment. She neither congratulated nor demurred, but went on with her household duties with the same method and precision as before. Men may come and go, hearts may be won and lost, republics may totter and empires may fall, but the grand scheme of sweeping, dusting, bed-making, and cooking knows no interruption. If I did not understand I at least commended this housewifely prudence, and often when the domestic battle was at its height I would spirit away my little charmer for the discussion of topics within my comprehension. At the outset I had declared that while it had pleased Providence to begin our romance in a burying-ground, I did not propose to sacrifice all tender sentiment to meditations among the tombs, and I bore her away to the old tree down by the river, where we sat for hours together as I unfolded my plans for our future life.

A man who has sat at the feet of the [Pg 82] philosophers from Ovid to Schopenhauer, and has gorged his intellect with the abstract principles of love, naturally adapts himself to the professorial capacity, and I soon saw that Phyllis, while one of the most lovable, one of the sweetest of girls, was almost wholly ignorant of the psychology of passion. I could not expect that a young girl of twenty-two would discourse glibly of the emotion in its intellectual phase, but I could not bear the thought that she should enter lightly into so serious a compact, and without gaining a reasonable comprehension of its mental analysis. Hence, as opportunity presented, I enriched her mind with the beauties of love from the standpoint of philosophers and thinkers, and showed her the priceless blessings that must result from a union dictated by careful provision of reasoning. To these addresses she listened with sweet patience, and if she did not always grasp their meaning, she showed much admiration for my erudition and frequently remarked [Pg 83] that she had no idea that love was so abstruse a science. It seemed to me, in the serenity of my years and the calm assurance of my love, that I was a most persistent wooer, and I was greatly grieved when she broke out rather petulantly one afternoon:

"I don't believe you really love me."

"You don't believe I love you? And why?"

She hesitated, half abashed by her own outburst, then added a little defiantly: "Well, in the first place, you never quarrel with me."

"And why should I quarrel with you? Aren't you the most amiable, the most perfect little woman in the world?"

"Oh, of course; I know all that. But I have always read, and always believed, that when two persons are truly, deeply in love, they have most exciting quarrels. Is it not true that in all romances the man is eternally quarrelling with the girl and bidding her farewell forever?"

"Yes, and coming back in ten minutes [Pg 84] to weep and grovel at her feet and beg her to forgive him. My dear little Phyllis, why should I bid you farewell forever, when I am morally certain that in half that time I should be cringing in the turf, weeping and begging you to say that all is forgiven and forgotten?"

"That would be lovely," she said pensively.

"Perhaps, but it would be very undignified and unnecessary. And I am not at all sure that you would admire me in that attitude even if I did imitate the heroes of romance. A weeping lover is much more agreeable in a novel than in actual life. However if you insist that we must quarrel, in order to demonstrate the sincerity of my affection, I shall suggest that we have our spats when we part for the night, in order that no precious waking hours may be lost."

"You are joking," she exclaimed with a little pout.

"Not at all. Still," I added reflectively, "even this plan has its disadvantages, [Pg 85] for if we quarrel when we part at night, it will necessitate my return to your window, which would not only annoy your aunt but might scandalize the neighbors. Furthermore it might give me a shocking cold, unless you immediately repented, for the nights are very damp. No," I sighed with great feeling, "all this seems impracticable. You must give me a better reason for my coldness."

Phyllis toyed with a clover blossom, and made no answer. I went on:

"As a slight indication of my unlover-like hauteur, let me confess that I am going to bring you a marvellously glittering bauble when I come back from the city, something that will bewilder you by day and dazzle you by night."

She shrugged her shoulders. "Of course you are; you are always giving me presents."

I laughed at this. "Well, suppose I am; I have never heard that it is a sign of waning affection to bestow gifts on the [Pg 86] loved one."

"You refuse me nothing. I dare say you would give me the Boston State House if I wished it."

"No, you are wrong there," I replied decisively. "If I bought the State House I should be compelled to include the emblematic codfish, and you know my aversion to codfish."

She smiled at the thought, recalling the Sunday breakfast, and then with a roguish look and a half-embarrassed laugh she said: "At all events you cannot deny that you did not kiss me when you left last night."

"Didn't I?" I asked in amazement, and then, quite thrown off my guard, I added thoughtlessly: "I had forgotten."

"That," she replied quietly, "was because you were so taken up with the philosophy of love, and the mental attitude, that you overlooked the physical demonstration. Do you remember the conversation?"

Unfortunately I did. I recalled that [Pg 87] I had spent an hour or more defining the moral status of love and proving the sufficing reason. It was not a pleasant reflection that so agreeable and instructive a conversation was not thoroughly appreciated.

"We spoke at length on love," I ventured feebly.

"That is, you did," she replied. "I'll admit that it was better than an ordinary sermon, because the subject was more personal. But don't you think we admitted the sufficing reason at the start, and isn't it natural that a girl who has been conventionally brought up is pretty well satisfied in her own mind of the moral status? Of course," she added, with a toss of her pretty head, "I am not asking you or anybody else to kiss me. I am merely curious to know if this plays any part in the philosophy of love as understood by the greatest thinkers."

Her speech had given me time to pull myself together. "No," I said with [Pg 88] marked emphasis, "I did not kiss you, because I had noted the unworthy suspicions you have expressed to-day, and I was hurt and grieved. It was hard for me to exhibit my displeasure in this way, and I am regretful now that I have learned that it was simply playfulness on your part. Don't interrupt. I am satisfied that the pure merriment of your nature is responsible for this assault, and I shall take great pleasure in making up this evening for the deficiencies of last night."

She laughed and we were friends again. And with such jocular asperities the days passed quickly and agreeably until my nephew arrived with the plans and specifications. Frederick Grinnell was not only my nephew, but an architect of reputation and promise, considering his years and experience. Like Phyllis he had been left an orphan early in life, and it had been my pleasure and privilege to give him an education and see that he was fairly started in life. While I think I may say that Frederick was not quite so attractive as [Pg 89] was I at his age, he was nevertheless a fine, manly young fellow, tall, well put together, of good habits, industrious and devoted to his profession. It pleased me to see that he admired Phyllis's pretty face and bright, animated manner; but one evening, when I fancied that he was too deeply stirred by her really beautiful voice, I took the opportunity to converse with him confidentially as we walked back to the tavern.

"I have been intending to tell you, Frederick," I began a little airily, "of the relations existing between Miss Kinglake and myself. So far it has been a profound secret"—I did not then know that the entire village was gossiping about it—"but I feel that I owe it to you, as my nearest relative, to admit that Miss Kinglake and I are engaged."

I paused, and noting that he did not wince or appear in the least degree discomposed, continued:

"Of course you will respect my confi [Pg 90] dence in this matter. Of course," I added magnanimously, "it will be perfectly proper for you to signify to Miss Kinglake that you are aware of our little secret as that will put us all on a better basis and lead to no misunderstandings. It would be awkward to play at cross purposes, and I should be extremely sorry, my dear boy, to think that I had withheld anything from you, for you have always enjoyed my fullest trust."

Whatever he may have thought, his manner betrayed no unusual interest. "I congratulate you," he replied very calmly.

Now that so perfect an understanding existed in the immediate family circle, I gave myself no further uneasiness. I was truly rejoiced to notice that Frederick was deferentially polite to Phyllis, and I encouraged him to show her those polite attentions which my betrothed would reasonably expect from my nephew. And at times I even insisted that he should represent me at certain gatherings of Phyllis's friends, who were too young and [Pg 91] frivolous to claim my serious attention. When he protested, and pleaded headache, business, or other sign of disinclination, I rallied him good-humoredly on his lack of gallantry.

"Nonsense, my boy," I argued; "a young fellow of your spirit should be only too glad to go out with a pretty girl and enjoy himself. You certainly would not deprive Phyllis of an evening's pleasure because your uncle has a stiff knee which interferes with his dancing, and—confound it, you know they never let me smoke at these frolics. Come now, be a good fellow and show the proper family impulse."

As they went off together I looked at them admiringly and rather fancied that I saw in them a suggestion of what Sylvia and I had been when we made the rounds of the birthday parties. For it is fair to confess that the image of Sylvia did not infrequently rise before me, and I constantly saw in Phyllis the replica of her adorable mother. In my happiest moments I [Pg 92] spoke of this suggestion to Phyllis, and continued to regale her with fragments of my early life associated with her family. At first I thought that the girl was somewhat piqued, fearing that Frederick was thrust upon her, although she admitted that he was good-looking, polite, and danced extremely well, but I succeeded in convincing her that true love should not be gauged by the low standards of hot-night dancing, and that all philosophers agree that the purest affection springs from quiet contemplation, such as I should enjoy while she was making merry with her friends. To this she once ventured to remark that in that case perhaps my affection would thrive to greater advantage if I contented myself with thinking about her and not seeing her at all, a suggestion which wounded me in my tenderest sensibilities, for I was very much in love. I was also not a little disturbed when, supplemental to my reminiscences, Mary went back to the past and humorously drew pictures of me as her own early [Pg 93] lover. There is considerable difference between the impalpable, airy spirit of the fancy and a wrinkled and austere feminine actuality of fifty.

In the midst of these innocent and improving pleasures a small cloud appeared in the summer sky. I received a letter addressed in a peculiar but not ornate hand, and I opened it with misgivings and read it with consternation.

Mr. Stanhope sir: Prudence and I thinks youd better come home. The plummer was hear twice yisterday and the cutworms is awfle. Hero got glass in her foot and the brown tale moths is bad again wich is al for the presnt.

Respecfuly

Malachy.

Duty is one of the exactions of life which I have never shirked when there seemed no possible way of evading it, but in this instance the call of duty was compromised by matters of equal urgency, for nothing can be more important than the successful administration of the affairs of love. It was a happy thought [Pg 94] that suggested to me a way out of the difficulty, which was neither more nor less than that we should all go to the city together. I sprang the proposition at a family conference. Phyllis was delighted. "There is always so much to be seen in the city," she cried, "and I shall meet Mr. Bunsey. It has been one of the dreams of my life to know a real literary man."

This appeared to call for an explanation. Heaven knows I am not jealous of Bunsey, and would not deprive him of a single distinction that is honestly his. But a regard for the truth, coupled with much doubt as to Bunsey's ability to live up to such lively expectations, compelled me to resort to a little gentle correction.

"My dear Phyllis," I said, "you must disabuse your mind of that fallacy. Bunsey is a popular novelist, not a literary man."

"But isn't a novelist a literary man?" she asked in amazement.

"Not necessarily," I replied pityingly. [Pg 95] "In fact I may say not usually. Of course we are speaking of popular novelists. The popularity of the novelist is in proportion to his lack of literary style. The distinctive popular charm of Bunsey is that he is not literary—at least, if he is, his critics have not succeeded in discovering it; he successfully conceals his crime. If he is popular, it is because he is not literary; if he were literary he could not be popular."

"That does not seem right," said my little Puritan.

"It is not a question of ethics at all, but a matter of taste. However, don't be prejudiced against Bunsey because he is a product of the time and fairly representative of the civilization. You shall meet him and shall learn from him how a man may succeed in so-called literature without any hampering literary qualifications."

Mary did not receive my proposition in a thankful and conciliatory spirit. She shook her head doubtfully, and when we were alone together, she gave voice to her [Pg 96] fears.

"Phyllis is country-bred," she said, "and knows nothing of the toils and snares that beset young girls in the city."

"Toils and snares," I echoed. "One might gather from your objections that we contemplate taking Phyllis to the city merely to expose her to temptation and corrupt the serenity of her mind. You seem to forget the elevating influences of my modest home."

"No, John; I dare say that your home is not objectionable, taken by itself. But I am not blind to the seductions of the great city. You too forget," she added, with a touch of complacency, "that I am not inexperienced or without knowledge of the profligacy of the town."

"Granting all this," I said, highly diverted by her earnestness, "and what are some of these seductions you have in mind?"

"Theatres," she replied promptly, "theatres and late hours, midnight suppers—and [Pg 97] cocktails."

I laughed uproariously. "My dear Mary, if these deadly sins and perils alarm you, we'll cut them out. I care little for theatres, and less for midnight suppers. And as for cocktails, I shall make it my peculiar charge to see that Phyllis never hears the abominable word. Allowing for the removal of these temptations, I still think that a trip to the city would do our country flower a world of good, though I have nothing but praise for the manner in which you have brought her up."

"John," she answered very gravely, "I have endeavored to do my duty as I saw it. I have tried to bring Phyllis up in the nurture and admonition of the Lord."

The expression carried me back to my childhood, and I bit my lips. "Of course you have," I said. "Wasn't I brought up in this same village, in the same way? Did not my good mother and my blessed, grandmother inflict nurture [Pg 98] and admonition upon me, that I might grow up as you see me, a true child of the pilgrim fathers? The nurture, I remember, was a particularly hard seat in our particularly gloomy old meetinghouse, and the admonition took up the greater part of the Sabbath day, with a disenchanting prospect of further admonition at home if I failed to keep awake. I do not mean to say that I am not thankful for the experience. In truth I am doubly thankful—thankful that I had it, and thankful that it is over."

To this Mary vouchsafed no further remonstrance than a distrustful shake of the head. Excellent woman! Is it not to such as you, earnest, faithful, self-sacrificing, God-fearing, that the best in young manhood, the purest in young womanhood, owe the strength of the qualities that are the vital force of the nation?

[Pg 99]

I **N** the end the united opposition was too much for Mary's arguments, and to town we went. The pleasure of the journey, on my part, was somewhat clouded as to the welcome we should receive from Prudence, and truly it acquired my greatest powers of dissimulation to feign an easy indifference and air of authority before that worthy creature, as with the most studied politeness and formal hospitality she received us at the gate. Prudence and I had sparred so many years that we were like two expert athletes, and while neither apparently noticed the other, each was perfectly conscious of the adversary's slightest movement. Hence I detected at once her strong aversion to Mary, whom she immediately selected as a probable mistress, and I saw her several times vainly try to repress a grimace of disdain and wrath. It was my first impulse to follow Prudence into the kitchen, after the ladies had gone to their rooms, and make a [Pg 100] clean breast of the untoward tidings, but I lacked the moral courage and contented myself with an inward show of strength. Why should I pander to this woman's caprices? Was I not master in my own house? Should I not do as I pleased? I would punish her with the severity of my silence, and perhaps in a week or two, when she was more tractable, I would condescend to tell her exactly how matters stood. In this I would be firm.

But the next morning, before my guests were out of bed, I decided that I was not acting wisely. Was not Prudence an old, faithful, and trustworthy servant? Had she not been loyal to my interests, and was not her whole life wrapped up in my comfort? Surely I wronged her to withhold from her the confidence she had so fairly earned, and the flush of shame came to my face as I reflected that I was indulging my first deceit. I took a turn in the garden, in the heavenly cool of the early morning, to compose my nerves for a very probable ordeal, and [Pg 101] then I walked boldly into the kitchen where Prudence sat, with a wooden bowl in her lap, paring apples.

It was one of the unwritten laws of the cuisine that Prudence was never to be disturbed when engaged in this delicate operation. She maintained that it destroyed the symmetry of the peel, and I dare say she was right. Consequently she looked at me reproachfully as I entered, and bent again more assiduously to her work. I was much flustered by the ill omen, but I knew that if I hesitated I was lost; so I advanced valorously, though with accelerated pulse, and said with all the calmness I could command:

"Prudence, I think it only right to tell you that I am going to be married."

One apple rolled from the bowl down along the floor and under the kitchen stove. I cannot conceive of any shock, however great, that would cause Prudence to lose more than one apple. Partly to conciliate, and partly to conceal my own [Pg 102] trepidation, I made a gallant effort to rescue the wanderer, and as I poked the hiding-place with my stick, I heard her say: "Lord, I know'd it'd come!"

"The fact that it has come, Prudence," I answered with a sickly attempt at gayety, "does not seem to be a reason why you should call with such vehemence on your Maker. There does not appear to be any need of Providential interposition. Things are not so bad as all that."

I always used my most elegant English when conversing with Prudence. If she did not understand it, it flattered her to think that I paid this tribute to her intelligence.

"Mr. John," she said, and there was a suspicious break in her voice, "for twenty years I have tried to do my duty by you, and now that I must go— "

"Go?" I interrupted; "who said you must go? Who spoke about anybody's going? You certainly do not expect to turn that bowl of apples over [Pg 103] to me and leave me to get breakfast?"

"No, Mr. John, I shall go on and do my duty, as I see it, until you have made all your plans and are comfortable."

"Now, look here, Prudence, I am very comfortable as things are, thank you. And you will pardon me if I say I cannot understand why you should go at all. I shall continue to eat, I hope, after I am married, and I think it altogether probable that I shall require a house-keeper and a cook. I believe they do have such things in well-regulated families."

"At my age, and with my experience, and considerin' how we have lived, Mr. John, I couldn't get along with a mistress, 'specially," she added with a touch of malice, "with a woman considerable older than me."

"Older than you? What are you talking about? Miss Kinglake is young enough to be your daughter."

Another apple rolled on the floor. "Miss Kinglake!" she exclaimed in astonishment, "that lamb? Good Lord, [Pg 104] I thought you were goin' to marry the other one!"

"Prudence," I said rather hotly, for I did not relish her amazement, "you will oblige me by not speaking of these ladies as the 'lamb' and 'the other one.' I might gather from your remarks that I am a sort of ravening wolf, instead of a well-meaning gentleman who is merely exercising the privilege of selecting a wife. But," I said, checking myself, for I was ashamed of my explosion, "I shall be magnanimous enough to believe that you are delighted with my choice, and that I have your congratulations. You will be glad to know that Miss Kinglake and I are perfectly satisfied with each other, and that we are both entirely satisfied with you. And now that we understand the situation, I think I may presume that we shall have breakfast at the usual hour this morning, and to-morrow morning, and for many mornings to come. And, by the way, Prudence, while I have honored you with my confidence, permit [Pg 105] me to impress it upon you that this revelation is not village gossip as yet, and you will put me under further obligations by not mentioning the circumstance. Good-morning, Prudence. Kindly call the ladies at eight o'clock."

And thereupon I hastily departed, leaving the good woman in a state of stupefaction, since, for the first and only time in our long and controversial association, had I retired with the last word. Taking a second turn in the garden I encountered Malachy, and my conscience reproached me. "Am I doing right," I asked myself, "in withholding the glad news from this faithful servant who has shown himself so worthy of my confidence? Is it not my duty to tell him—not so much to interest him in his future mistress as to demonstrate the trust I repose in him?"

Malachy received my confidence with less excitement than I had expected. In fact I was slightly humiliated by his seeming lack of gratitude. He touched his [Pg 106] hat very respectfully, and observed irrelevantly that the roses below the arbor were looking uncommonly well. This was a poor reward for my attempt at consideration, and further convinced me of the uselessness of establishing anything like intimate relations with the proletariat.

"By the way, Malachy," I said in parting, "you will keep this matter a profound secret. Miss Kinglake and I are desirous that we shall not be annoyed by village chatter and premature congratulations."

Having discharged my duty to my good servants, I felt that my obligations, so far as the relation with Phyllis was concerned, were at an end, and the morning wore away without further misgivings of disloyalty. In the afternoon Bunsey came over for his daily smoke, and as we sat together in the library, and I noticed the entire absence of suspicion in his manner, my heart smote me. "Truly," I reasoned silently, "I am behaving ill to [Pg 107] an old friend who has never withheld from me the very secrets of his soul. Should I not be as generous, as outspoken, with him as he has always proved to me? Should I not confide to him this one precious secret, at the same time swearing him to preserve it as he would his life?"

I blew out a ring of smoke, and then I began with the utmost seriousness: "Bunsey, how do you like the ladies?"

He shifted his position, tipped the ashes from his cigar, and replied tranquilly: "Oh, I dare say I shall in time."

The answer vexed me. Bunsey was a bachelor, and should have been therefore the more impressionable. I forgot for the moment, in my annoyance, that he was a novelist, and had been so diligently creating lovely and impossible women to order that he was not easily moved by the realities of humanity.

"At all events," I replied with delicate irony, "I am glad that the future is [Pg 108] hopeful for the ladies. My reason for asking the question was simply to lead the way to a confidence I intend to repose in you. To proceed expeditiously to the end of a long story, I intend to marry one of them."

Bunsey's tranquillity was unshaken. "Which one?"

"Which one?" I echoed with heat, "why, Miss Kinglake, of course."

"Does she intend to marry you?"

"Naturally."

"Or unnaturally?"

"Confound your impertinence!" I roared, "what do you mean by that?"

"No impertinence, at all, my dear fellow. In fact it is most pertinent. Miss Kinglake is a girl, and you—well, you voted for Grant."

"Which is your gentle way of saying that I am too old."

"No, not too old; just old enough—to know better."

"We are never too old to love," I said, conscious that I was uttering a melancholy [Pg 109] platitude.

"Too old to love? Heaven forbid! But we may be too old to marry—at least to marry anybody worth while. Come, Stanhope, tell me: do you really love this young woman?"

"Love her? Here I have been telling you that I intend to marry a charming girl, and you turn about and ask me if I love her. Of course I love her. I have been loving her in one way and another for years."

"What do you mean by that? I thought you only met her a few weeks ago."

I smiled pityingly. "So I did, but for years she has been my affinity. Incidentally I don't mind saying I began by loving her mother."

Bunsey sat up straight. "Oh, you loved her mother. Was her mother pretty?"

"She was as you see Phyllis. In fact I think she was, if anything, a trifle prettier. We were playmates and schoolmates, and in the nature of things, if I had not [Pg 110] wandered off to the city, I presume we should have married. Dear little Sylvia," I went on musingly, "I can see her at this moment, looking down from heaven and smiling on my union with her daughter. For if ever a match was made in heaven this was. Confound it! what are you doing now?"

While I was talking Bunsey had reached over, taken a sheet of paper and was busily writing. He looked up carelessly.

"Your story interests me, and is such good material that I thought I would make a few notes. Young boy loves young girl—goes to city—forgets her—young girl marries—has charming daughter—dies—years pass—venerable gentleman returns—sees daughter—great emotion on part of v. g.—thinks he loves her—proposes—accepted—mar—no, there I think I must stop for the present."

"Oh, don't stop there, I beg," I said sarcastically; "if you are thinking of using these materials for one of your popular novels, be sure to throw in a few duels, [Pg 111] several heartrending catastrophes, and other incidents of what you call 'action,' appropriately expressed in bad English."

Bunsey was imperturbable. "Thank you for your appreciative estimate of my literary style," he replied coolly; "but really, my consideration for my old friend deprives me of the pleasure of robbing his diary."

I was still out of temper. "Bunsey, I don't mind favoring you with a further confidence. You're an ass!"

With this parting shot I strode out of the library, when, remembering the sacredness of my revelation, I turned back.

"Of course you will understand, Bunsey, that however flippantly you may choose to regard what I have said to you, you will have the decency to keep the subject-matter to yourself. I do not ask your congratulations or your approval, but I demand your secrecy."

"The ass brays acknowledgments," answered Bunsey meekly, helping himself to another cigar. "You may rely on my [Pg 112] loyal and devoted interest. The fact that I have heard your secret twice before to-day shall not open my lips or cause me to violate your trust."

Notwithstanding my attitude of indifference I was greatly troubled by Bunsey's unfeeling suggestion. Could it be possible that I had mistaken my own heart? Was I, yielding, as I had believed, to the first strong passion of my life, only deluding myself with a remembrance of my vanished youth? I dismissed the thought impatiently. For, after all, was not Bunsey a hopeless cynic, a fellow without a single emotion of the ennobling sentiment of man toward woman, a sordid story-teller, who created characters for money, wrecked homes, committed literary murders, played unfeelingly on the tenderest sensibilities, and boasted openly that the only angels were those made by a stroke of the pen and retailed at department store book-counters? And while thus reasoning Phyllis came to me, so winsome in her girlish beauty, so radiant in the happiness [Pg 113] I had infused into her life, so joyous in the pleasures of the present, that I laughed at my own doubts, reproached myself for my own unworthy suspicions, and straightway forgot both Bunsey and his evil promptings.

[Pg 114]

L **OVE** at eight and forty is a very [Pg 115] pleasant and indolent emotion, marking the most delightful stage in the progress of the great human passion. At twenty-five we talk it; at thirty-five we act it; at forty-five it is pleasant to sit down and think about it. The very young man loves without really analyzing. Ten years later he analyzes without really loving. In another decade he has compounded the proportions of love and analysis, and becomes, under favoring conditions, the most dangerous and hence the most acceptable of suitors. The man in middle life takes his adored one tolerantly, and keeps his reservations to himself. In the ordinary course of events he has acquired a certain knowledge of feminine character, he knows the rocks and the shoals of love, and, skillful pilot that he is, he avoids them. He is sure of his course, master of his equipment. If he errs at all—but [Pg 116] I anticipate.

Those were very joyous days, notwithstanding the applications of cold water so liberally bestowed by my confidential advisers. And eagerly and successfully I exerted myself to convince the doubting ones in general, and Bunsey in particular, how absurd were their suspicions, and how apparent it was that Phyllis and I had been purposely created for each other. Mary threw herself into our pleasures as heartily and joyously as her New England nature would permit, which was never a very riotous demonstration, and Phyllis, with the effervescence and enthusiasm of girlhood, eagerly assented to every proposition that had its pleasure-seeking side; while I, as a thoughtful lover should, busied myself in schemes for summer dissipation, thankful that it was in my power to prove so devoted a knight, and inwardly rejoicing at my triumph over those who had taxed me with such unworthy thoughts. Even Frederick—good fellow that he [Pg 117] was—allowed himself unusual days of vacation to partake of our merriment, and it pleased me greatly to see that when business cares or physical disinclination kept me off the programme, he no longer allowed his indifference to interfere with his duty as my nephew and personal representative. Such, I take it, is the obligation of all young men similarly placed.

For, before many weeks had passed, I discovered that it was not wise to allow the fleeting dissipations of the moment, however alluring, to monopolize time which should be given to the serious affairs of life. I found that a cramped position in a boat in the hot sun brought on nervous headaches, and that too much time in the garden when the dew was falling was conducive to lumbago. Furthermore I had been invited by a neighboring university to deliver my celebrated lecture on the protagonism of Plato, and several new and excellent thoughts had come to me which required [Pg 118] careful and elaborate development. I explained these matters conscientiously and fully to Phyllis, and while she offered no unreasonable protest, her pretty face clouded, and she did me the honor to say that half the enjoyment was removed by my absence. Once she even went so far as to declare that Plato was a "horrid man," and that she believed I thought more of him than of her—a most ridiculous conclusion but so essentially feminine that I forgave her at once. And, when she came to me, and put her arms around my neck and urged me to go with her to a tennis match—a foolish game where grown-up people knock little balls over a net with a battledore—I pointed out to her that such spectacles, while eminently proper for young folk, argued a failing mind in those of maturer years. With a charming pout she said:

"Do you think you would have refused to go if my mother had asked you?"

Now tennis is a sport that has come [Pg 119] up since Sylvia and I were children together, but I recalled, with a guilty blush, the time when she and I won the village championship in doubles in an all day siege of croquet, so what could I say in my own defence? Therefore I went with Phyllis to the tennis-court and sat for two long and inexpressibly dreary hours watching the senseless and stupid proceedings. It was pleasant to reflect that I was with Sylvia's daughter, and I tried to imagine that the keen interest of youth still remained, but I was sadly out of place. I am satisfied that this game of tennis has nothing of the fascinating quality of croquet. On our arrival home Phyllis kissed me, and thanked me for what she called my "self-denial," but after that one experience Frederick represented me at the tennis-court, as, indeed, the good-natured boy consented to do at many similar festivities.

And so the summer wore gradually away, one day's enjoyment lazily following [Pg 120] another's, with nothing to disturb the serenity of my life, or to interfere with the calm content into which I had settled. Phyllis was everything that a moderate and reasonable lover could wish—kind, gentle, affectionate within the bounds of maidenly discretion, attentive to my wishes, and considerate of my caprices. The more I saw of her the more I was persuaded that I had chosen wisely and well. One afternoon—Frederick, at my suggestion, had gallantly given up his work in the office and taken Phyllis down the river. I sat with Bunsey in the library, and took occasion to expound to him the philosophy of perfect love.

"The trouble is," I said, "that people rush blindly into matrimony. They think they are in love, work themselves up to the proper pitch of madness, propose and marry while they are in delirium. Hence, so much of the wretchedness and misery that we see in the homes of our friends. For my part I am committed to the doctrine of affinities. It is true that I, like [Pg 121] many others, was guilty of the usual folly in my youth, and perhaps that gave me the wisdom to wait for my second venture until precisely the fight party came along. Matrimony, Bunsey, is an exact science. If we regulate our passion, control all silly emotion, study feminine nature as critically and methodically as we investigate a mathematical problem, and commit ourselves only when the affinity presents herself, we shall make no mistakes. For, after all, what is an affinity? Nothing more than a human being sent by Providence as perfectly adapted to the wheels and curves of your nature."

"A very pretty theory," retorted Bunsey, grimly; "and, by the way, when do you think of rushing into matrimony?"

"Really," I said, somewhat confused, "to be entirely honest with you, I have not settled on any particular day. You see Phyllis should have her fling. She is very young."

"True, but you are not."

As Bunsey said this he rose and tossed [Pg 122] his cigar out of the window. "Stanhope," he went on, "we are old friends, and I don't wish to be continually seeming to interfere with your business, but if I were a man with fifty years leering hideously at me, and engaged to a pretty girl of two and twenty, I'd make quick work of it before Providence came along with a younger affinity in a Panama hat, negligée shirt, and duck trousers."

I stared at him with a sort of helpless amazement. "Exactly what do you mean?" I asked.

"Well," he answered, shrugging his shoulders, "at the risk of being kicked out of the house, let me say that I think such an affinity has already presented himself."

"Indeed, and who may that be?"

"Suppose we say Frederick."

"My nephew?"

"Exactly; your nephew. He is an uncommonly good-looking fellow, and, thanks to his uncle's childlike belief in Providence and the doctrine of affinities, [Pg 123] he has most unusual opportunities to test that doctrine for himself. I dare say that he is making a formal study of the situation at this very moment, and inviting Providence to appear on the scene as his sponsor."

What more was said at this interview, if, indeed, it did not terminate with this brutal statement, I cannot recall, for Bunsey, usually so flippant and cynical, spoke with an earnestness that stunned me. My knowledge of the philosophy of love told me that he was wrong; my observation of the actualities of life made me fear that he might be right. Theoretically, I could not have been mistaken in my course; practically, I began to see weak spots in the chain of evidence. Swiftly, I ran over the events of the spring and summer, and as little spots no bigger than a man's hand magnified themselves into black clouds, Bunsey, sitting opposite, seemed to grow larger and larger, and his smile more malicious and demon-like. Possibly, had I been a younger and more impetuous man, [Pg 124] I should have flown into a passion, taken Bunsey at his word, and kicked him out of the house; but the philosophy of the thing engrossed me, filled me with half fear, half curiosity, and engaged all my mental faculties. Had I been mistaken? Could I be deceived in the daughter of Sylvia?

However strong my suspicions may have been, they were not increased when, with the evening, Phyllis and Frederick came home from their excursion. Never was Phyllis more unreserved, more cordial, more joyous, more attentive to the little wants, which I, in a mean and shameful test, imposed on her. She could not be acting a part, this New England girl, with her alert conscience, her Puritan impulse and training, her aversion to everything that savored of deceit. And Frederick was as much at his ease as if I knew nothing, as if I had not heard of his duplicity, as if the whole house and grounds were not ringing with accusations of his unworthiness. Such are the phenomena [Pg 125] of the philosophy of middle life, I insisted that he should remain for the evening, and, after dinner, with that contrariness accountable only in a true student of psychology, I made a trifling excuse and walked down to the square, leaving them together.

The curfew was ringing as, returning, I entered the lower gate at the end of the garden, and passed slowly along by the arbor. It may have been Providence, it may have been chance, it certainly was not philosophy that directed my steps to the far side of the syringa hedge which shut me off from the view of those who might come down to the rustic seat at the foot of the cherry tree. At least I had no intention of playing the spy, and when I heard Frederick's voice, and knew instinctively that Phyllis was with him, I quickened my pace that I might not be a sharer of their secrets. But an irresistible impulse made me pause when I heard the foolish fellow say:

"After to-night I shall not come again. [Pg 126] It is better for us to break now than to wait until it is too late."

Her reply I could not hear. Presently he said, and a little brokenly:

"I have fought it all out. It has been hard, so hard, but I must meet it as it comes."

Then I heard Phyllis's voice: "It is for the best."

"I believe that you care for me. I know how much I care for you, and how much this effort is costing me. We were too late. No other course in honor presents itself. God knows how eagerly and hopelessly I have sought a way out of this tangle of duty."

Again I heard Phyllis's voice, sunk almost to a whisper: "I have given my word; it is for the best."

"The governor has been so good to me," Frederick exclaimed resentfully, "that I feel like a criminal even at this moment when I am making for him the sacrifice of a life. He has been my father, my protector. What I am I owe [Pg 127] to him, and I must meet him like a grateful and honest man. You would not have it otherwise?"

And for the third time Phyllis answered: "It is for the best."

Had I been of that remarkable stuff of which your true hero is made, of which Bunsey's heroes are made, and had I come up to the very reasonable expectations of the followers of literary romance, I should have burst through the syringa with passion in my face and rage in my heart and precipitated a tragedy. Or, on the other side, I should have taken those ridiculous children by the hand, and ended their suffering with my blessing then and there. But as I am only of very common clay, with little liking for heroics, I did what any selfish and unappreciative man would have done, and stole quietly away. I even felt a sort of fierce joy in the knowledge of the security of my position, a mean exultation in the thought that Phyllis was bound to me, and that those from whom I might reasonably fear the [Pg 128] most, acknowledged the hopelessness of their case. Most strangely there came to me no resentment with the knowledge that I had been supplanted by my nephew in the affections of the girl; the fact that she loved another surprised rather than agitated me. My argument was upset, my doctrine of affinities had been seriously damaged in my individual case, and here was I, who should have been yielding to the pangs of disappointment, or raging with wounded pride, reflecting with considerable calmness on the reverses of a philosopher.

I went into the library and lighted a cigar. I threw myself into an easy-chair, and as I looked up I saw a spider-web in a corner of the ceiling. "I must speak to Prudence about that in the morning," I said to myself with annoyance. Then for the first time it came to me that I was out of temper, for I am customarily tranquil and not easily upset. My mind wandered rapidly from one thing to another, and oddly enough I [Pg 129] caught myself humming a little tune which had no sort of relevancy to the events of the day. I tried to dismiss the incident of the garden as the temporary folly of a romantic girl, which would wear itself out with a week's absence. Why should it trouble me? Had I been lacking in kindness or affection? Should I be disturbed because a few boat rides and the influence of moonlight had wrought on a mere child? Was I not secure in her promise, and had I not heard her say she had given her word? As for Frederick, was he not my debtor? Had he not confessed it? Then why give more thought to the matter? It was awkward, but both were young and both would outlive it. Sylvia and I were young, and we outlived it.

But still kept ringing in my ears that despairing half-whisper: "It is for the best."

Petulantly I threw away my cigar and went up to my room. I walked over to the dressing-case and turned up the gas. The shadow displeased me and [Pg 130] I lighted the opposite jet. Then I stood squarely before the mirror and looked critically at the reflection.

Yes, John Stanhope, you are growing old. That expanding forehead, with the retreating hairs, tells the tale of time. The gray upon your cheeks is whitening and the razor must be used more vigilantly to further deception. Those creases in your face can no longer be dismissed as character lines; the shagginess of your eyebrows has the flying years to account for it. Plainly, John, you and humbug must part company. You are not of this generation and it is not for you.

I turned down the gas, threw open the window and let the moonlight filter in through the elms and over the tops of the little pines. The soft beauty of the night soothed me, and gradually and very gently my irritation and annoyance slipped away. Why should not a young girl, radiant in youth and beauty, affect a young man of her generation? What [Pg 131] has an old fellow, with all his money and worldly experience and burnt-out youth, to give in exchange for that intoxication which every girl may properly regard her lawful gift? Undoubtedly I should make a better husband, as husbands go, than my romantic nephew, and any woman of rare common sense would see the advantages of my position, but why burden a woman with that rare common sense which robs her of the first and sweetest of her dreams? No, John Stanhope, go back to your pipe and your books and your gardening, your life of selfish, indolent do-nothing. Take life as it comes most easily and naturally. By sparing one heart you may save two.

And that nephew of mine—what a fine, manly fellow he proved himself when put to the test! The governor had been good to him and he was going to stand by the governor. How my heart jumped, and what a warm little feeling there was about the internal cockles as I recalled his words. Bravely said, my [Pg 132] boy, and nobly done! I fear I should not have been so generous at your age, and with Sylvia—

And with Sylvia! How the past crowded back at the thought of her! Who are you, old dreamer, who neglected the gift the good gods provided in the heydey of your youth to return to chase the phantom of the past? Behind that little white cloud, sailing far into the north, Sylvia may be peeping at you, and smiling at the delusion of her ancient wooer. Or why not think that she is pleading with you—pleading for her child and the lover, as she might have pleaded for herself and somebody else, had somebody else known his own heart before it was too late?

I watched the white cloud as it passed on and on, growing smaller and fainter as it receded. I settled back still deeper in my chair and sighed. And then—O unworthy knight of love!—and then, I fell asleep.

[Pg 133]

I **N** the morning, before the family was astir, I wrote a note, pleading a sudden and imperative call to town, and vanished for the day. I argued with myself that such a step was a delicate consideration for a young woman, who, having listened to a confession of love a few hours before, would be hardly at her ease at a breakfast-table conversation. Incidentally I was not altogether sure of myself, although I was much refreshed by an excellent night's sleep which comes to every philosopher with courage and strength to rise above the unpleasant things of life. If Phyllis had yielded to an emotion of grief, there was little trace of it when we met at evening. I fancied that she was somewhat paler, and her manner at times seemed a little listless, but otherwise there was no great departure from her usual demeanor. As for myself the long sunshine of a summer day and the conviction that at last the opportunity had come to me to play the rôle [Pg 134] of a minor hero gave me a peace that amounted almost to buoyancy. No need had I of the teachings of the musty old philosophers reposing on my bookshelves. John Stanhope had learned more of life in a few short hours than all his tomes could impart. His books had helped him many times in diagnosing the cases of his friends; when John fell ill they mocked and deceived him.

Opportunely enough Phyllis followed me into the library, and when at my request she sat on a little stool at my feet, and I held her hand and stroked her soft light hair, a pang went through my heart, for I felt that she might be near me for the last time. The philosopher had yet much to learn. For several minutes we were both silent. Of the two I was doubtless the more ill at ease, though I concealed it bravely.

"Phyllis," I said at last, "did you ever get over a childish fondness for fairy-stories?"

She smiled at this—was I wrong [Pg 135] in fancying that her smile was that of sadness?—and answered: "I hope not."

"Because," I went on, bending over and affectionately patting the hand I held, "a little fairy-tale has been running through my head all day, and I have decided that you shall be the first to hear it and pass on its merits. And because," I added gayly, "if it has your approval I may wish to publish it. Shall I begin?"

She nodded her head—I could swear now to the weariness the poor child was so staunchly fighting—and looked off toward the sunset.

"Once upon a time—you see that I am conventional—there lived a beautiful young princess, on whom a wicked old troll had cast an evil eye. Now this wicked troll was not so hideous as the trolls we see in our fairy-books—I must say that—but he was so wicked that even this deficiency could not excuse him. The princess was as young and innocent—I was going to say as simple—as she was [Pg 136] beautiful, and the wicked troll talked so much of his experience in the world, and boasted so hugely of his wealth and generosity and other shining virtues, that the imagination of the poor little princess was quite fired, and she was flattered into thinking that here was a treasure not to be lightly put aside. And so, in a foolish moment she consented to be his bride, and he took her away to his castle—I believe trolls do have castles—to make ready for the marriage. While the preparations were going on, and the wicked old troll was laughing with glee to think how he had deluded a princess, a handsome young prince appeared on the scene, and what so natural as that the princess should immediately contrast him with the troll. And it came about, also quite naturally, that before the prince and the princess knew that anything was happening, they fell so violently in love with each other that the birds, and the bees, and the flowers in the garden, and the squirrels in the trees sang and hummed [Pg 137] and gossiped and chattered about it."

Here I paused. Phyllis did not look up, but I felt a shiver run through her body as I stroked her hair and put my arm around her shoulder to caress away her fear.

"But it happened that although the princess was so much in love that at times she must have forgotten even the existence of the old troll, she was still possessed of that most inconvenient and annoying internal arrangement which we call the New England conscience, and one night, when the prince had declared his love with more ardor than usual, she remembered the past, how she had promised to marry the troll, and how she must keep her word, as all good princesses do. And the prince, who was a very upright young man, most foolishly listened to her, and agreed to give her up. Whereupon these poor children, having resolved that it was for the best— "

Phyllis looked up quickly. Her face was white, and a look, half of fear, half of [Pg 138] reproach, came to her eyes. She sank down and hid her face in her hands. Both my arms were around her and I even laughed.

"Dear little princess," I whispered, "don't give way yet. The best is still to come. For you must remember that this is a fairy-tale and all fairy-tales have a good ending. And, to make a long story short, this wicked old troll was not a troll at all, but a fairy-godmother, who had taken the form for good purposes. I would have said fairy-godfather, but I have never come across a fairy-godfather in all my reading, and I must be truthful. Well, the fairy-godmother came along right in the nick of time—and, of course, you know who married and lived happily ever after?"

The convulsive movement of the poor child's body told me she was weeping. And I, being a philosopher, and more or less hard-hearted, as all philosophers are, let her weep on. Presently she said in a voice hardly audible:

"I gave you my promise and I meant [Pg 139] to keep it. I am trying so hard to keep it."

"Of course you are, little girl, but why try? A bad promise is far better broken than kept, and, come to think of it, I am not at all sure that I am anxious to have you keep it. How do you know that I am not making a desperate effort to secure my own release?"

She raised her head quite unexpectedly and caught me with the tears in my eyes. My eyes always were weak. "Why, you are crying!" she said.

"Of course I'm crying. I always cry when I am particularly well pleased. It is a family peculiarity. You should see me at the theatre. At a farce comedy I am a depressing sight, and that is the reason I always avoid the front seats."

Then realizing that I might be carrying my gayety too far, I went on more soberly:

"Can't you see, Phyllis, that the old fool's romance must come to an end? Don't you understand that had I the selfish wish to hold you to a thoughtless [Pg 140] promise, our adventure would terminate only in misery to us both? Perhaps you and I have been the last to see it, I, because I was thinking too much of myself, you, because you were carried away by an exalted sense of duty. Thank heaven it is clear to us both now. For it is clear, isn't it, dear?"

The foolish girl did not reply, but she kissed my hand, and it is astonishing how that little act of affection touched and strengthened me.

"So we are going to make a new start and begin right. To-morrow I shall see Frederick and make a proposition to him, and if that rascal does not give up his heroics and come down to his plain duty as I see it—well, so much the worse for him. No, don't raise objections"—she had started to speak—"for I am always quarrelsome when I cannot have my own way. Go to your room and think it over, and remember," I said more gently, for that old tide of the past was coming in, "that you are Sylvia's [Pg 141] daughter, and that Sylvia would have trusted me and counselled you to obey me in all things."

Slowly and with averted face Phyllis rose and walked toward the door. I had commanded her, and yet I felt a sharp pang of bitterness that she had yielded so quickly to my words. It seemed at the moment that everything was passing out of my life; that Phyllis, that Sylvia, that all the once sweet, continuous memory was lost to me forever. I could not call her back, and I could not hope that she would return. Philosopher that I was I could not explain the sinking and the fear that took possession of me. The philosopher did not know himself. All his thought and all his reasoning could not solve the simple riddle the quick intuition of a girl made clear.

She had reached the door before she paused. Then she turned. I had risen mechanically and stood looking at her. As slowly she came back and waited as if for me to speak. And when the dull [Pg 142] philosopher groped helplessly for words and could not meet the appealing eyes, she put her hands on his shoulders, and laid her warm, young face on his heart, and said, "Father!"

The night was peacefully beautiful. I had strolled out of the garden and down to the river, and there along the bridle-path on the winding bank I walked for miles. Absorbed in my own thoughts I gave no heed to my little dog, Hero, trotting at my side and looking anxiously up at me with her large brown eyes, as if saying in her dog fashion: "Don't worry, old man; I'm here!" A strange, inexplicable happiness had fallen to him who thought he knew all others, and did not know even himself. I crossed the river to return on the opposite shore, and all the way back, through the arching trees, the shadows danced in the moonlight and the crickets chirped merrily. Life seemed so contrary, so bewildering, for I thought of the wedding [Pg 143] music in those early mornings at my boyhood home, and I wondered at the optimism of Nature in attuning all emotions to a joyous note.

Again in my garden I saw a half-light in Phyllis's room. Coming nearer I saw that she was standing at the window, with the same cloud on her face that had betrayed the battle with her conscience. At sight of her all the joyous emotion of my new tenderness overwhelmed me and I cried out cheerily:

"Good-night, Phyllis!"

Something in my voice sent a smile to her eyes and gladness to her heart, as, half leaning from the window, she kissed her hand to me and called back softly: "Good-night, father dear!"

The south wind came, bringing the scent of the rose and the honeysuckle, and stirring the drowsy branches of the elms. The river rippled merrily in the moonlight, hurrying to bear the tidings of happiness to the greater waters, and [Pg 144] off in the distance the blue hills lifted their heads above the haze. Toward the north scudded the friendly little white cloud, and it seemed again a soothing fancy that Sylvia—

O sweet and pleasant world!